Heart to Heart

Love's Brew Series

BLUE SAFFIRE

Perceptive Illusions Publishing
Bayshore, New York

Blue Saffire/Perceptive Illusions Publishing, Inc.
PO BOX 5253
Bayshore, NY 11706
www.BlueSaffire.com

Ordering Information:
Quantity sales. Special discounts are available on quantity purchases by corporations, associations, and others. For details, contact the "Special Sales Department" at the address above.

Heart to Heart/ Blue Saffire. -- 1st ed.
ISBN 978-1-941924-36-5

The heart has to be willing to go through the healing process for the healing to take place.

—BLUE SAFFIRE

CHAPTER ONE

Meddling Kids

Jack

"I'm your father. I don't have to answer to you. I said I'm not ready," I snap at my sons.

They don't understand it's not easy to move on after loving the same woman for thirty years. I'm fifty-one. I don't know the first thing about dating in this day and age.

"Dad, you can't lock yourself up in this house and wither away," Chance says.

"I can do whatever the hell I want. I have a business to run. I'm not about to start running around looking for love when I have a legacy to keep going."

"Dad, we're not telling you to ignore the business. Stop being so dramatic. Chance and I have the business covered anyway. All we're saying is that you should consider going on a date or two.

Miss Fantan has been asking you to have dinner with her for months."

"And I haven't been ready for months. Your mother was the love of my life. Why can't you boys understand that? She was your mother."

"Dad, hear us out."

"No. I'm done with this conversation. Leave me be."

"Hershel," Chance says as he places a hand on his brother's shoulder. "Let it go."

I nod my head. Finally, they're getting it through their thick heads. I'm growing really tired of them butting into my life. I've lived a hell of a lot longer than they have. I know what it's like to love and lose. They don't know shit.

If they did, they wouldn't be badgering me like this. I lost my best friend, the love of my life. My wife was everything a man could ask for.

When my father handed the brewery house and the land over to me, my Lisa was right there with me to turn this place into something of my own.

It was her idea to turn this place into a destination. I built the B&B with my own hands while these two were in the womb and in diapers.

"Damn brats."

Coral

My divorce is final, and I need something new in my life. I've been thinking of a move, but I don't want to settle anywhere I'll regret. This is why my daughter and I will be visiting a little town I want to check out.

Jo is a good girl and she's been my support system as I've gone through my divorce from her father. Ralph and I are still friends. We just fell out of love. People change, life changes, you grow apart.

"Okay, mom, the car is all packed," Jo says. "If we leave now, we can make it in time for the beer flights and burgers at the B&B. I love that dress and scarf on you, by the way."

I look down at the yellow dress with its high low circle skirt and flirty cup sleeves. I tossed the light blue scarf on in case I get cold during the drive. The gold flats took me the longest to decide on. I didn't know how far I wanted to step out of my comfort zone.

I touch my natural curls. Jo gave me an amazing twist out. My coils look bold and shiny. I'll never be able to get it this way myself.

"Thanks," I say as I brush my hands down my dress then pick up my purse. "This place has such a cool concept. I can't wait to get there. I heard the entire town is lovely and has a lot of unique spots like the Brewery and B&B," I reply.

"Yeah, I have a list of places to check out during our visit. It seems like a cool place to live. I'm excited for you. The best part is that I wouldn't be too far away if you decide to buy a place there. I mean, six hours isn't bad."

"Only because you love to drive. I just hope I like the library and the staff. That will play a big part in my decision as well."

"I have a good feeling about this. I want to see you happy again. You deserve it."

"Honey, I wanted to thank you. I know this hasn't been easy for you. Your father and I didn't want to stick you in the middle of things."

She waves me off. "I honestly think you two did the best thing for you both."

I cup her face and kiss her forehead. "You're the greatest thing to come from my marriage. I don't regret a thing. Let's go."

"I'm driving."

I smile and hand her the keys. Ralph and I raised an amazing human. This we both can be proud of.

CHAPTER TWO

Checking In

Jack

These old bones are tired. I toss my legs over the side of the bed and stretch. The aches and pains of old age are real. I think back to my days in high school. I was the captain of my football team.

I look down at my middle today. I'm a long way from that strapping young man. I'm not out of shape, but I'm packing on a lot more pounds than I was back then. I don't think I'll ever get back the abs and muscles I had in my youth. The only way I'll see that physique in the mirror ever again will be if I'm looking at one of my boys.

I look at the clock and snort. Yet another sign of my age. I need my midday nap.

The buzzer goes off, letting me know new guests have arrived. I run a hand through my hair before reaching for my glasses and placing them on.

"Time to get back to work," I mutter to myself.

I get up and amble from my room to jog downstairs and greet our guest. The boys should be outback getting the afternoon event set up. Chance does the grilling and cooking, and Hershel gets the flights of beer set up.

"Welcome to Harrington's. Do you have a reservation with us or are you here for lunch?"

"We have a reservation for Coral and Jo Marks."

I look up at the sound of the sweet voice and freeze in my tracks as my gaze meets with some of the most expressive eyes I've ever seen. They're set in a pretty brown face.

I clear my throat. "Ah, yes, you have a two week stay booked." My face burns with a blush. I don't know what's wrong with me.

"Does your husband need help getting the bags to the room?"

"Oh, no. It should be two rooms. And Jo is my daughter. She went back to the car for something. She should be right in. She'll help me with the bags."

"No, no. I'll be happy to help you ladies upstairs," I rush out and grab two room keys.

"Do I need to sign in or anything?"

"Um, you can come see me after you settle in."

I want to palm my forehead. I don't know what's wrong with me. You'd think I'd never seen a woman before. I'm never this discombobulated or out of sorts.

I grab a few of her bags and start for the stairs. "You can follow me."

She looks at the door and then turns to follow me. I get to the stairs and start up. "Breakfast starts at eight, the brewery opens at one, but we do offer lunch around noon—"

I trip up the stairs, but her bags break my fall. I don't think I've ever been more embarrassed in my life.

"Are you all right?"

"Pop."

"Oh no, is he okay?"

"I'm fine," I grumble as I brush Chance off me as he tries to help me up. My face burns with embarrassment.

"Jo, help me with these bags," Coral says.

I can't even look the woman in the face. I turn to her daughter and hand over the keys. Like mother like daughter, she's a pretty little thing as well. Most likely, the reason Chance can't tear his eyes off her.

"Chance, help them to their rooms."

He snaps out of it. "Oh, right, um, Jo, I have those. I'll get them settled in and come back to check on you, Pop."

"I'm fine." I rub the back of my neck. Then murmur to myself. "My pride is the only thing bruised."

Coral

I feel so bad for the handsome innkeeper. I stand frozen as Jo and his son walk by with our things and start up the stairs. He won't look at me, and I want to see those deep blue eyes again.

His thick gray hair gives him a distinguished look. I'm forty-eight. He doesn't look to be much older than me. I reach out and touch his forearm.

"I do hope you're okay. Jo is a massage therapist. Do let us know if there's anything we can do."

"Thank you, ma'am. I'm fine. Just an old fool with a hurt ego."

"You don't look that old to me and trust me. I fall all the time."

He snorts. "Darling, I'm fifty-one. I'm sure you have a long way to go before you're complaining of old age and falls in front of strangers."

I give him a smile. He looks damn good for fifty-one. "Between you and me, I'm forty-eight. I'll be there sooner than you think."

He finally lifts his head fully, displaying his towering height. I'm five-six. This man has to be six-three maybe six-four. His broad shoulders are appealing. Those eyes, they are so intense and mesmerizing even behind his glasses.

"Mom, these rooms are so charming. Come on up."

"Excuse me …"

"Jack, the name is Jack."

I stick my hand out. "Coral. Now we're no longer strangers."

He takes my hand, and sparks fly. I haven't had this feeling in years. He searches my face as he holds my hand in his big rough one. I can't help but wonder what it would feel like against other parts of my skin.

"Mom," Jo groans like she's still a teenager.

"I hope to see you later, Jack. I'll need a few friends if I'm going to live around here.

His eyes light up. "You thinking of moving into town?"

"If it feels right."

He nods. "I'll let you get to it. Enjoy your stay. I'm sure we'll see each other around."

CHAPTER THREE

Disaster

Jack

"Hey, Uncle Jack, the beer tastes great and these new beer fries and the beer cheese in the burgers, man, amazing. I think this place is keeping our little town going."

No thanks to your daddy. I think to myself. My brother-in-law is a pain in the ass. Leave it to him and this town wouldn't exist. Not like we know it.

However, I keep my disdain to myself. Lord knows my nephew has become a better man than his father. Not that the man will allow the boy to forget where he comes from.

"I don't know if I would say that, but thanks, Mayor."

"Come on, Uncle Jack. I told you to stop calling me that."

"It's who you are, isn't it?"

He releases a sigh and frowns. "Yeah, all right. I see the new potential librarian is staying with you. I sure do hope she takes the position.

"So many of our kids depend on that place. Heck, I remember when Chance, Hershel, and I used to use that place to study and hide out from our chores." He laughs.

I pat him on the shoulder. "You boys have always been a pain in my ass."

I shake my head and head over to the table where our new guests are. So Coral's looking to become the new librarian. Gorgeous and smart. I was intrigued from the moment she said she might be moving into town.

I don't miss the fact that Chance and Hershel are already seated with our guests. I'm about a few feet away when Lauren, one of the young waitresses bumps into me with a tray of beers.

No doubt, because she couldn't take her eyes off Hershel. The little thing has been sweet on him for years.

I groan. Why is the universe hell-bent on me looking like a fool in front of this woman?

"Oh, Mr. Harrington, I'm *sooo* sorry," Lauren says with wide eyes.

I brush a hand down my front and shake it out. "Don't worry about it," I grunt.

I take the towel she hands me and turn for the house. So much for trying to be suave and redeem myself. I run a hand through my hair. Maybe this is my Lisa telling me this isn't the time.

Coral

"Oh, no," I breathe in concern. "Is he okay?"

"He will be. Pop's a tough one. Although he seems a little out of it today."

"He was so embarrassed earlier. I feel so bad."

"What happened earlier?" Hershel asks.

The two boys have been charming. I believe Jo has gained both of their attention. They're both as handsome as their father.

Chance even has a dimple in his left cheek. Something I noticed about his dad earlier.

"Your dad tripped up the stairs."

"What?" Hershel says and looks at his brother. "Maybe I should go check on him, being the doctor in the family and all."

"Don't be so full of yourself. You're a Vet," Chance says and snorts.

"You know I've been thinking about going into pediatrics or something that will get me in an OR."

"Oh, I used to date a surgeon. It didn't work out. The long hours and all," Jo says.

"Yeah, that's why I'm leaning toward pediatrics. I love kids and want to start a family of my own. It would be good to have time for them and my wife."

"I'm sticking to the family business. I want to expand this place. You know, make it a real retreat. Maybe bring in a massage therapist for the whole spa vibe and add some yoga classes or something. A place to get away and relax," Chance says.

"Oh, that would be awesome. I'd have a little getaway when I come to visit Mom," Jo replies.

"Yeah, sure."

I have to cover my mouth to keep from laughing at Chance's defeated response. I think he hoped Jo would be interested in being that therapist he wants to hire. My daughter will miss a clue thrown at her face. I've watched it a million times.

I stand because it doesn't look like either boy plans to go check on their father. I leave Jo to figure out she has two new suitors. They both seem to be sweet young men.

CHAPTER FOUR

Sparks

Jack

"What's wrong with you, Jack?" I chide myself for fussing with my hair.

I don't normally put any of this shit in it, but the last time Phil cut my hair, he used this pomade and styled it. I got a lot of compliments, and he gave me some to try at home.

"What am I doing?" I breathe as I look into the mirror.

My chest is covered in gray hair and my gut is fuller and firmer from all the beer.

I flex my pecs. I still have it there. They're the only definition still in tack. Coral is a beautiful curvy woman. I'm sure she's not interested in this dad bod, yet I'm still standing here like an uncertain teenage boy trying to figure out what to wear.

If I'm honest with myself, it has been lonely. The boys have lives of their own. I wouldn't mind someone to spend time with and Coral has been the first woman to remind me I'm still a man.

I'd all but given up on a sex life. Lisa was too ill in the end for us to make love. As I said, I haven't been attracted to much of anyone else. Not until now. I'd fuck the glow off that skin.

"Jesus, what's wrong with me? Get it together, Jack. She's just a woman," I mutter and head to the closet for my blue button-up.

I shove my arms in the sleeves and head out of my bedroom. If it kills me, I'm determined to make a better impression tonight. What is it they say? Be careful what you ask for.

Coral

I yelp as I run into the hard body of none other than Jack. He wraps an arm around me to keep me from falling backward down the stairs, almost tumbling down with me. I reach out and press my hands to the walls.

"Damn it," he growls as he steadies us both. "I'm so sorry. You must think I'm some kind of clumsy idiot."

"No, not at all."

I can't take my eyes off his bare chest peeking out from beneath his open shirt. He's not ripped, but he's solid. I bite my lip and look up into his concerned blue gaze.

I clear my throat. "I came to check on you, but you look fine to me."

"I'm a widower. Lost my wife a year ago. I have two boys.

"Chance and Hershel. This place has been in my family for four generations. It seems like we expand it in some way with each.

"I haven't been with a woman in two years. You're the first I've been attracted to since I lost my wife. Oh God, why can't I shut the fuck up?" he says with a blush and pained expression on his face.

I cup his cheek and look into his eyes. "Jo is an only child, although I raised my nieces after my sister passed, and the three grew up like sisters. Mel and JC are traveling the world at the moment. I'm newly divorced and looking for a change. I'm here to consider the head librarian position in town.

"You're a very attractive man. It's been almost three years since I've been intimate with anyone. Your rambling is adorable, by the way."

He cups my face and kisses me. I'm totally surprised by the heated kiss. I'm even more surprised when he palms my ass and presses me into the door he came out of. I reach into his shirt and claw my fingers up his back, causing him to groan.

When he palms my breast, I whimper into his mouth. "Oh God," I cry as he moves his lips to my neck.

"You're so beautiful."

"All right, Pop."

Jack freezes and groans, turning to look down the stairs. When I follow his gaze, I find Jo with a smile and a wide-eyed goofy look on her face, Chance and Hershel with proud smiles on theirs, and the mayor …

"Kill me now."

CHAPTER FIVE

In Denial

Coral

"Don't you have a room of your own you should go to?" I say to Jo as I roll my eyes.

She's been relentless since catching me and Jack kissing. I'm already embarrassed enough. I'm here for a job and the mayor of this small town—of all people—caught me in a lip lock with a man I barely know.

What kind of first impressions is that? Jack is a very attractive man, but I need to pump the breaks on all of this. I haven't even committed to the job or the move.

I wouldn't want to hurt the man if this isn't my place. I also want to stay because it's the right place for me. Not because I started a fling with the first man I've met here.

"Mom, come on. I saw that kiss and the heated stares after. He seems like a nice man. Maybe this is your place. What if fate has drawn you here?

"I'm just saying. Don't shut this all down because you're a little embarrassed. Mayor Washington is nice, and Jack happens to be his uncle."

I groan and palm my face. "That knowledge doesn't make me feel any better. Good night, Jo. I will see you tomorrow."

"Oh, right. Your interview is in the morning. That's the only reason I'm leaving. We will talk more about this tomorrow."

"Not if I can help it," I murmur under my breath.

Jo hops up off my bed and comes to pull me into her embrace. I sigh and hug her back. I know she means well.

At her age love and romance is one big fairytale filled with stars and excitement. I've long since been disillusioned about relationships. They take work and patience on both ends.

I'm starting over again. This time I want to think about the things I want and need. A partner is just that … a partner. Not someone who's required to fill in my holes and gaps, but someone to complement the cracks and kinks I've already mended along my journey.

This is one of the things I've learned from my marriage and divorce. I don't know that a widower is ready for that role. Jack may need something totally different from what I need.

"Stop overthinking things, mom. There's nothing wrong with getting to know the man."

"Says my daughter who doesn't realize she has not one, but two young men interested in her," I chuckle and shake my head.

"Huh?"

"Exactly," I snort.

Jack

"Pop, what are you doing? Where are you going with that bag?" Chance asks.

I purse my lips and allow my nostrils to flare. I'm about sick of these kids. Who told them they run my life? I have shoes and hairs on my ass older than they are.

"I'm heading to the cabin to do some fishing. You boys have been getting after me to have some fun and take time to relax. Well, here it is. You two can handle this place for a few weeks," I grumble.

"Do you mean two weeks? Pop, come on. I know you're not about to run away after that kiss," Hershel says.

"That was totally inappropriate. I'm not some damn teenager with no home training and raging hormones. Your grandmama would have tanned my hide. Mrs. Joni still might kick my ass."

"Mrs. Joni would be happy to see you happy. Don't do this, Pop. Miss Marks seems like a nice woman. Give this a shot."

"If it's meant to be, I'll see her around after she accepts the job and then I can get to know her properly."

"Dad—"

"Leave it alone, Chance," Hershel says.

"Come on. We can't let him do this. He just said he wasn't ready. That kiss looked like he was ready to me."

"Clearly, I'm not ready. Look at what I did."

"You didn't seem like you were alone, Pop. She was right there with you."

I close my eyes as images of the kiss fill my head. I can still feel her soft body against mine. The flavor of her mouth was heavenly.

"Nope, that's why I need to go. You boys know how to reach me if you need anything. I'll see you in two weeks," I say and shake my head.

Opening my eyes, I take my bag and head out. This is the right thing to do. If this is meant to be, I will get to know Coral when I return.

If she's still around, coward.

CHAPTER SIX

Spring Valley

Coral

"This is probably inappropriate to say, but you're by far my favorite candidate. Your knowledge and disposition are all the things I had in mind for the new hire. We have such a great community here and you'll fit right in," Flo, the retiring head librarian says.

She's a precious little old woman with an infectious smile. She has kept me laughing and smiling since the start of the interview. I had my doubts when I woke this morning.

Especially after heading down for breakfast to learn Jack took off last night. I don't want to complicate the man's home. I had hoped we could talk and see where things could go if we slowed down.

"This is such a wonderful library. The town is charming too from what I've seen so far. May I ask what your plans are after retirement?"

"Oh, dear. That's one of the reasons I'm so happy to have found you. You don't seem like you will chase me away.

"I'm only retiring because these bones can't keep up any longer. I don't think you'll be able to drag me away from here though. I plan to continue with Storytime and the arts and crafts programs," she says with a sparkle in her hope filled eyes.

"I would love to have you around. Storytime. That's for the preschoolers, right?"

"Yes, dear and the elementary kids who love to sit in. I usually read to them in the afternoons. A lot of our working parents from Spring Valley and North Folk—the town over—bring their little ones in for the childcare. It's been a thing since I was a little girl. It's how I fell in love with books and this place."

"I love that. I fell in love with books much the same way. If I do take the position, you're always welcome here. I'm counting you as my first friend in town," I say with a smile.

Her eyes light up. "In that case, tell me what I need to do to get you to stay and accept the job."

"I guess, house hunting would be next on my list. If I find someplace that feels like home and speaks to me then I'm more likely to accept."

"Oh, then I better introduce you to Betty-Lou Fantan. She's our local realtor. I'm sure she'll find you the perfect fit."

"I would appreciate that. Thank you so much."

She gives a soft laugh and waves me off. "You're staying at Harrington's for now, right? Betty-Lou will jump at anything that will get her in front of our strapping Jack Harrington. I swear the woman was waiting with bated breath for our poor Lisa to take her last breath."

I feel a pang in my chest. I have no right to be jealous. The man has run away from me.

However, the thought of another woman vyning for his attention causes that little green monster to lift its head. I'm too old to be petty and I need a home if I want to take this job. I've fallen in love with the library already.

This might be my place after all. With that in mind, I shrug the jealously off. Jack can date whoever he likes.

"Hey, Flo. I'm here to drop Emma off. I didn't see anyone out front."

"Hello there, Mayor Cash. Have you met Coral Marks? I believe we have our new head librarian."

"That's great. You have no idea how much we need you. Flo is the best, but she could sure use some help around here. This library means a great deal to our community.

"Not to mention, it was great to see my uncle interested in someone of the opposite sex since my aunt passed. I know it's only been a year, but I can't help but feel like we lost her long before that.

"For me it was like losing them both. You let me know if there's anything I can do to make your transition here smooth and easy. I know Chance and Herschel will be happy.

"Jo has made quite the impression on those two. She's a lovely young woman. If I were younger, I'd be in the running as well." He laughs.

"Oh my," Flo gasps.

"What? What did I say?" The mayor says with wide eyes.

"I just offered to introduce her to Betty-Lou. I thought she would be able to help her find a place. I didn't know Jack was … you know."

The mayor groans. "It's probably better if I help you find a place. I used to be a realtor. I still have a few connections. Some listings came to my email just the other day."

"I don't want to be a bother," I say.

"Trust me, you'll want my help and it's no bother at all."

I frown to myself wondering who this Betty-Lou is and what the fuss is about. Not wanting any drama to influence my decision, I decide to allow the mayor to help me.

"Okay, if it's not too much trouble. Thank you, Mayor Washington."

"Please, none of that. Call me Cash. It's no trouble at all. You just tell me what you're looking for and I'll get right on it. I have some time in my schedule tomorrow. I can show you a few places then."

"I'll need at least four to five bedrooms. I want all my girls to feel welcome to come stay with me and have their own space to do so. The extra bedroom would be for my home library.

"One to two bathrooms, and a nice kitchen. JC loves to cook. If you can fit some type of bonus room for our chocolate and wine nights and the potential to start our book club back up, that would be awesome."

"You have more daughters?" he asks and lifts a brow.

"JC and Mel are my nieces, but I've raised them so they're more like my daughters. I've had them since my sister passed."

"Oh, you two have something in common," Flo says.

I look to her questioningly. Mayor Cash clears his throat, pulling my attention. I turn to him and find a sad smile on his face.

"My brother and his wife were killed by a drunk driver. I had Emma that night babysitting for them while they had a date night. Em has been with me ever since."

"Oh, I'm so sorry for your loss. Please let me know if there's anything I can do to help. I know how overwhelming things can become at times. They were so young when it happened. How old is your Emma?"

"She's eight going on thirty," he chuckles. "This place is a great help. Emma loves to come here for the crafts and Storytimes."

"I can't wait to meet her."

He glances down at his watch and pulls a face. I'm sure he has plenty to do. I feel bad for taking up so much of his time.

"I'm sure she's going to love you. I'll get on those listings. Sorry, ladies, but I do have to go. Miss Marks, if there is anything you need, and I do mean anything, don't hesitate to let me know."

"Thank you so much, I'll keep that in mind."

"Flo, Pop will be by for Emma today. He's coming in from business. Miss Coral, let me be the first to welcome you to Spring Valley," he says.

I don't get a chance to correct him. However, as he says the words this begins to feel more like home. I stare after him and wonder if his uncle will be as happy to have me here.

Quickly, I shake off the thought and rub my hands on my thighs. If I find a place that suits all my needs, then I'll know this is home. I won't jump the gun just yet.

"He's going to find you the perfect place. I just know he is," Flo gushes.

"I hope so."

"Come, I'll introduce you to Emma."

"Sounds good. I'd like that."

Jack

"My man," Terry croons as I walk into his bait shop. "What have those boys of yours done to get you out here on my side of town. You haven't been out here since ..." He trails off and swallows down his next words.

He's right, I haven't been this way since before I lost my wife. It's been about two years. The year I spent by her side and the year that I've been grieving her loss.

"I don't know if I can blame it on the boys this time," I say and force a smile.

"Well, whatever chased you this way, I'm glad for it. It's good to see your face. It will be nice to get some fishing in with my old buddy."

"That's what I'm looking forward to. Need to get my thoughts together."

"Oh yeah? Give me a bit to get this place handled and I'll be right with you. There's still time to get some good fishing in today.

"Sounds good to me. I'm going to grab a few things before we head out."

"That's fine by me. It's all my treat."

"You don't have to do that."

He scoffs and waves me off. I move to find the items I need to replace. The tension has finally begun to leave my body.

I chided myself the entire ride here. I almost turned back to sit down and talk with Coral. She needs to know this isn't the man I am.

I would like to take her on a proper date and get to know her. If she gives me a chance, I'll keep my hands and lips to myself.

"How have you been?" I call out as I look through the hooks and try to find my favorite brand of line.

"To be honest with you, buddy, things have been a mess here. Them folks been trying to buy me out. Your brother-in-law hasn't been any help. He's in cahoots with those sons of bitches.

"He ought to be mourning his sister like you are. Damn fool," Terry growls.

I shake my head. I've heard about all the trouble he's been having around these parts. This land has been in his family longer than my land has been in mine.

If those developers break him, they'll be moving into town for mine. My brother-in-law Courtland is a self-serving asshole. His own children haven't wanted anything to do with him for years.

He and Lisa even had a falling out before she died. She wouldn't tell me what it was about, but it was enough for her not speak to him ever again. It's the only thing I've ever seen the bastard regretful over.

"You hang in there. Don't let them folks strong arm you into shit. Cash is doing his best to make sure his daddy and those scumbags don't come in here and turn our little town upside down."

"Oh, you can bet your ass I'm not selling out. They can all kiss my natural Black ass."

I chuckle and walk my items over to the counter. I'm sure Terry will give them hell before he sells this land. I can't say I blame him.

"Norton is on his way to run the shop for the rest of the day. I'll meet you at the dock."

"I'll get us some lunch and beers."

"Sounds good to me."

***

Terry sighs, causing me to look up from the spot on the boat that I've been staring at. He's looking right at me, surely seeing way more than I want him too. My thoughts have been back at the B&B with a certain woman.

"I've known you for a long time, Jack. Something is on your mind. Would you like to talk about it?"

"Yes and no," I grumble like a spoiled child.

"All right. In that case, I'll wait you out. We ain't going nowhere anytime soon, so I'm ready when you are."

I sit silently, while I gather my thoughts and feelings. This is what I came for, to clear my head. I know Terry will give it to me straight.

"How long did it take for you to be ready to date after losing Marly?" I blurt out.

Terry sits back and narrows his gaze on me. It's an accessing look, not a judgmental one. Terry lost his wife about five years ago.

He's been on a few dates that I know about. Although he's currently single. Terry is a handsome guy. He has an inviting smile, and his brown skin always seems to shine.

"I'll be straight with you. Even after going on my first few dates, I don't think I was ready. I couldn't even try for the first two years," he says after a few beats.

His eyes grow distant before he shakes his head and continues. "I wouldn't have if not for the kids pushing me to. It's not the same, you know? We met Marly and Lisa in high school. That woman is all I've ever known. I guess if the right one comes along that might change things, but it ain't easy, my friend."

I nod. As I get ready to speak again, I feel a tug at my rod. I jump up to reel my catch in. A smile comes to my face, it feels good to be out here.

I almost forgot how much I love fishing. The fresh air, the peace of it all. In my grief, I've let go of a lot of things that once brought me joy.

"What makes you ask about dating?" Terry asks after I place my catch in the cooler and cast my line once again.

I shrug. "I might have met someone," I murmur.

"Well, I'll be. Did Betty-Lou Fantan finally get her hooks in you?"

I scoff. "No. You know better than anyone. That's never going to happen."

"You don't let Betty-Lou hear you say that." Terry shudders with a wince.

I chuckle. "She's new to town. Well, she's considering moving here. Her name is Coral Marks. She's interested in the librarian position."

"I heard they had a few candidates in the running for the job. This Coral must be something to have you all tied up like this."

"That she is. I can't put my finger on it, but I was smitten at first sight. I … I just don't know how to do this anymore.

"I want to hide behind losing Lisa but that sounds weak at best to my own ears. Especially after what I did last night. I'm an old fool."

"What the heck did you do last night? I feel like I'm missing some details here."

I groan and pull a hand down my face. I can feel her in my arms. It wasn't a question of if I should leave, I had to leave.

"I embarrassed myself, that's what I did. I damn near mauled the woman. I don't know what came over me."

Terry begins to chuckle. I glare at him and purse my lips. This isn't a laughing matter.

"If the woman wanted to, she could press charges against me," I mumble.

"I'm sorry. It's just ..." He pauses to get his laughter under control. "I've never seen you like this. Not even in high school. You were always so confident and went after what you wanted. I mean, it sounds like you did go after what you want, but this ... regret? The unsure energy, that's not you at all."

"Shoving my tongue down a stranger's throat isn't me either. I've been off since the little thing and her daughter checked in." I shake my head.

"Well, tell me more about her. What does she look like?"

I bite my lip and smile. My thoughts go right to those pretty expressive brown eyes. Her smile is imprinted in my brain.

"She's ... how do I explain her. Remember that crush we had on Pam Grier. How I used to drool over her movies? Man, I thought she was the prettiest thing walking.

"Coral has that same smooth confidence about her. She's breathtaking. Marly would have gone crazy over those lush, full coils."

I stop to think about that. Terry's wife was a hairdresser. Women used to come from two and three towns over to come see her and get their hair done. She loved what she did.

I lick my lips as I think more about Coral. "Her skin looks so soft. It feels even better. She smells like coco butter and raspberries."

"Wait a minute. You're talking about a sister, aren't you?"

"Yeah, she's a gorgeous Black woman. The total opposite of Lisa, but man, I can't stop thinking about her."

"I'm assuming she's still at the B&B, so why are you here?"

"Because I made a complete fool of myself. If I'm here with you, I can't be there trying to stick my tongue down her throat like a horny old bastard."

"Jack, Jack, Jack," he chuckles and shakes his head. "If I'm right, it's been over two years since you've been with a woman. You're still a man. So you got a little ahead of yourself.

"Now, that lines up with the Jack I know. You've always gone after what you've wanted. This ... this ... I don't even know what to call it. My old friend wouldn't run from anything. Especially not a pretty woman.

"My Marly was faithful to me, but you always had a way of making her and every other woman who came in contact with you blush. Where's that suave, confident guy? I know better than anyone how much you've been hurting.

"Heck, then again, I can't claim to know anyone else's feelings, but what I do know is that you and I know firsthand that life is short. Tomorrow isn't promised to either of us. If this Coral has made you feel something then you should explore that.

"This ache may never go away but having someone to soothe it while you're still here living this life ain't hurting no one. You're a good man, Jack. You did more for Lisa than most would. You were by her side until the very end.

"I don't reckon she would fault you for finding love again or at the very least, having someone in your life to remind you you're a man and it's okay to feel like one," Terry says as he holds my gaze.

"Well, shit."

"You're going back, aren't you?"

I pull a hand down my face. "Yeah, I'll head back in the morning. I owe you a catfish dinner before I leave."

"You're my best friend, so I'm not going to hold you to that. We can raincheck that dinner."

CHAPTER SEVEN

Welcome Wagon

Coral

"Grandpa," Emma squeals and jumps up from the table I've been sitting at with her.

She's such an adorable little girl. I've enjoyed reading with her this afternoon. I'm getting such a good vibe from this place. I can totally see running this library.

I turn to find a handsome older gentleman who dips to pick Emma up in his arms. He stands with her on his hip as he smiles up at her. Emma wraps her arms around his neck and gives him a squeeze.

"How's my princess doing?" he croons.

"I'm having such a good time with my new friend. Miss Coral is so pretty and smart. I like her," Emma sings.

"Miss Coral, huh? I think I should meet this new friend," he says as he looks over to where I'm sitting.

I stand and give a polite smile. He moves closer with Emma still in his arms. Then he stretches out his hands.

"You must be this Miss Coral the whole town is buzzing about. They weren't lying about how gorgeous you are. I'm Courtland Washington, this little beauty's grandpa. If you can believe that," he says and winks at me.

Goodness, the men in this town are handsome. However, noticing how handsome Emma's grandfather is makes me think of Jack. That kiss left one hell of an impression.

I can't help but wonder what made him leave. Quickly, I shake off my disappoint and focus. I didn't come here to get involved with anyone.

This is a fresh start. I want to know who I am without being married or raising children. I've spent more of my life being those things to others and have forgotten what it's like to be something to myself.

Yes, Jack taking off was for the best.

I take his hand. "It's very nice to meet you. I haven't been here long so I'm not sure you've heard much about me."

He brushes his thumb over the back of my hand as his smile lights up his face. It's a smooth move, subtle but intentional. As is the way he pins me with his stare.

"News gets around fast in this town. I'm sure you'll find that out soon enough." He winks at me.

Something about his words unsettles me. I'm well aware that this is a small town. Flo shelled out quite a bit of gossip in the small time we spent together.

However, I hadn't thought to allow that to sway my decision. I live a pretty boring life. I'm not sure I'll give them much to talk about.

I pull my hand back and look around for Flo. I think it's time I return to the B&B. I'm sure Jo can't wait to hear about how my interview went. I want to see how her exploring has gone.

"Oh no. I think that might have come off wrong. I hope I haven't put you off to our little town."

"No, no. My interview was over hours ago. I should get back to the B&B before my daughter begins to worry."

"Right, you're staying with my brother-in-law and nephews."

"Oh yes, my daughter did mention that the mayor is Jack's nephew."

"Jack?" He lifts a brow. "I didn't know you were so familiar with my brother-in-law."

My cheeks heat. "Well, I'm not. He told me and Jo to call him Jack."

His expression turns to one of disappointment. "Is Jo your husband? Rumors made it seem as through you were single."

"Jo is my daughter. It was nice meeting you. Sweetheart, I hope to see you around," I say to Emma.

"Did you drive over?" Courtland asks before I can take off.

"No, I left the car for my daughter to explore."

"Well, in that case you have to allow me and Emma to drop you off."

"Thank you, but I don't want to be a bother. I'll be fine."

"Nonsense. It's no bother at all. I've been craving one of their burgers and a beer anyway. I had plans to head over to the brewery already."

"Come on, Miss Coral. We'll get you to Uncle Jack's. We can finish our book chat. I wanted to hear what you thought about the end. I was so surprised," Emma says as her eyes light up.

My heart fills with warmth. Children like Emma are the reason I love what I do. I can see in her face that she's off on an adventure in her head.

"When you put it that way … I guess it's better than walking," I relent.

"You were going to walk from here?" Courtland says with surprise written all over his face.

"Yeah, it would have given me a chance to learn more about the town and how to get around."

He looks me up and down. "You would have had blisters all over your pretty little feet." He then chuckles and his eyes light as if he's in a distant memory. "I remember the day Lisa tried it. Jack hadn't come to the library for movie day, and she wanted to check on him.

"The problem was my daddy didn't want her dating, and she thought she was keeping secrets. Well, Daddy found out about them, and she wasn't supposed to go out to the farm.

"This was before it was a B&B. Daddy didn't even have to tan her hide. The road did it for him. She couldn't walk for three days. Daddy didn't even bother punishing her."

"Oh no, did she at least get to check on Jack?"

"He's the one who found her hobbling up the road. He got her in his truck and brought her home. That was the day I knew my sister was in love.

"The way she looked at him. That boy was her hero. There wasn't a thing my daddy was going to be able to do about it. Five years later, she was pregnant and married.

"Jack never had eyes for anyone else. It was always Lisa for him. We've all been lost over the last year, but I know my brother-in-law has taken it the hardest," he replies.

I look down at my feet and begin to fidget with my hands. Maybe that's why Jack took off. The poor man is still grieving his late wife.

My stomach growls, filling in the sudden silence. Courtland chuckles again. I look up to find him watching me.

"Looks like I'm not the only one who could use one of those burgers. Let's get you on out of here."

I'm hungry and could use a glass of wine or one of the beers. I sigh and nod. I have some thinking and planning to do.

Jack

I look up as Jo and the boys walk in. Her laughter fills the air and warmth fills the room. She has a light about her just like her mama.

"Pop, what are you doing back here?" Chance asks.

"I had a change of heart after talking with Terry and doing some fishing. Decided to come on back."

"You and your mama finding everything to your liking? Is there anything we can do to help?" I ask Jo not wanting to just come out and ask about her mother's whereabouts.

"I'm fine, sir. Mom has been out on her interview all day. I sort of don't want to text and disturb her. Although I'm starting to get a little worried. Then again, this is Mom. She probably got wrapped up talking about books and catalog systems."

"Can I fix you something to eat? Brought back some catfish."

She pulls a face before carefully schooling her expression. "No thanks. I'm not big on seafood. I'm actually going to head up to shower and change. Chance and Hershel have offered to take me to the old theater. I'm excited to check it out."

"All right then. You kids be safe."

"Actually, only one of us can go. It's my night off. Hersh, I think that means you'll have to go next time," Chance says with a smug smile.

"You know what? I've got it. Y'all can go. I have dinner service covered with the staff. Those new cameras you guys insisted on will help me man the front desk if I need to jump in to help out."

"Oh, wait. You guys made it seem like you had time. We don't have to do this tonight," Jo says. "I'll just do some reading and wait on Mom."

"You young folks go on and have a good time. I'll wait for your mama to come back. I'll shoot Flo a text to see if she knows what's the hold up. Don't you worry about a thing."

"That's so nice of you, Mr. Jack. I really don't want to be a bother."

"Are you sure, Pop?" Hershel asks.

"Yeah, it will be fine. I'll text one of you to let you know when Coral returns."

"Pop, you text? Come on now," Chance snorts.

"If you don't get."

The boys chuckle and shake their heads. I narrow my gaze at them. Jo has a smile on her face.

"One of you guys should start a group text to help him out," Jo says.

"I know how to send a darn text. I said get. All three of you."

The boys chuckle as they drag a snickering Jo along with them. I shake my head, one of my boys is about to have his heartbroken. They just don't see it yet.

"Oh, um, sir. Is Hershel leaving?"

I roll my eyes as Lauren appears at my side. The disappointment in her voice could be heard by a deaf man. If that smitten look on Hersh's face means what I know, Lauren is in for a rude awakening.

"Yeah, he's taking the night off to go to the theater with Chance and Jo. Is there anything I can help you with?"

"No, I've got it. She's pretty, ain't she?"

"That she is."

"I wish I could get him to look at me like that," she murmurs to herself and turns to leave.

I open my mouth to say something but the sound of tires moving across the gravel catches my attention and I decide to bite my tongue. A glance at the camera tells me it's Courtland's SUV.

Emma jumps out the back, and a smile comes to my face. However, what sends my blood boiling is when Courtland rounds the truck to open the door for Coral to step out. I have no right to be jealous or angry, but I still ball my fists at my sides and go to step outside.

Irrational, I know. Especially after leaving last night, but Courtland is an asshole and he's no good for Coral. He's the last man in this town she needs to fall in with.

"Thanks for the ride. I owe you one. I hadn't realized the distance until the ride here. I never would have made that walk," Coral says as she looks up at Courtland.

"Anytime. I told you it wasn't as close as you thought." He winks at her. "How about having a beer and a bite with me. That will make us even."

I don't know what comes over me. I step up behind Coral and place my hands on her hips. The gesture reads of the possessiveness I feel.

Courtland frowns as he takes us in. Coral cranes her neck to look back at me with a smile on her lips. I'm so tempted to crush these sweet lips with mine. However, I restrain myself from doing so.

"I promised Jo I'd keep her mama company while she and the boys head to the theater. You're welcome to get that beer and bite but you'll be doing so with Emma," I say more tightly than I intend to.

"Maybe some other time then," Courtland responds.

"Um, well, I haven't decided if I plan to take the position or move here. It's a lot to think about. Maybe if I do intend to stay, I can buy you your next burger and beer," Coral says, not looking away from me.

"Or maybe I can show you what all Spring Valley truly has to offer to help persuade you into becoming a permanent member of our lovely community," he croons.

"Now why would you be interested in that when you've done nothing but try to dismantle our home for the last three years."

"Perception, perception. You say dismantle; I say progress into the future. If you all would take the time to listen to the full proposal, then everyone would see how this will help the community."

"Listen, I don't want to cause any drama. Thank you, Courtland. Emma, I'll see you around, sweetheart," Coral says and steps out of my hold to head inside.

I turn to look after her. She looks as gorgeous as she did when she arrived. I get the feeling I just messed up.

I want to go after her to fix this, but I feel Courtland's gaze on me. I turn and glare back at him. Emma has taken off no doubt to order dinner and a milkshake. We placed them on the menu just for her.

"My sister has only been gone a year. What in the hell do you think you're doing? I thought the rumors were bullshit when I heard you were sniffing around the potential new librarian.

"I have to admit, she sure is pretty, but you have some nerve. What the hell do you think people are going to say? Do you plan to ruin her reputation before she even settles in?"

"What I plan to or don't plan to do with my life is none of your damn business. Your sister knew I was faithful to her up until her very last breath. Something your ex-wife can't say about you.

"Get your selfish ass off my property before I throw you off. I know what you've been up to. It ain't right what you're trying to do to this town and your own damn son."

"My son is stuck in the past like the rest of you. This town needs new life breathed into it. Why not allow the Bradley Group to come in and make the changes that will get us all there?"

"Because it ain't their home. Those of us who were born here, who's people were born here—we're a family. You just don't do family the way you're trying to do this town."

"Change is good, Jack. Look at what you've done with this place. Your family's farm has survived because with every generation change has happened but look around you.

"There aren't as many original businesses and families still in this town. People are moving on but they're not coming back. Nor are we pulling in new blood. The Bradley Group can change all of that," he growls at me.

"I know change is good but not like this. You know this town won't survive those folks. They're going to pick this place apart and then what?

"Have you thought about Emma or Cash or the real future of this town that doesn't line your pockets? Have you thought about anybody other than yourself?"

"I could ask you the same when it comes to Coral. What about your boys? Did you think about how they would feel to see you dating some other woman?"

"We'd be damn fine with it," Chance replies, his voice booming in the air.

"I know I'm good as long as Pop is happy. Sounds like you're the only one with a problem. What happened? Pop got to her before you could run her out of town with a broken heart?" Hershel says.

"I didn't see a ring on her finger. Which means I'm still in the game. Besides, I'm the better option since we all know you're still mourning my dear sister," Courtland bites out.

"Sir, I don't know you, but please stay away from my mom. I will hurt you," Jo says.

It doesn't miss my notice when Chance slips his arm around her shoulder and guides her toward his truck away from his uncle. If I weren't so spitting mad, I would laugh. Instead, I head back inside to see if I can find Coral and salvage the mess I've made.

CHAPTER EIGHT

I'm Sorry

Coral

"Just a minute," I call as someone knocks on my room door.

With all that drama going on last night, I decided to order dinner up to my room. Clearly, Jack and his brother-in-law have some bad blood between them. I didn't want to be caught in the middle of any of that.

Jo sent me a text to let me know she had gone out with Chance and Hershel to the local theater. I took the alone time to get some reading done and weigh my options. I do like Spring Valley, and I love the library and the fact that Flo intends to stick around.

If not for the male drama, I'd be all in. However, two men having a pissing match over things I know nothing about isn't going to sway me from doing what's best for me. I intend to go house hunting and see if a home calls to me.

Then and only then will I make my final decision. My ex-husband and I made some sound decisions financially during our marriage and I was able to walk away with plenty of money to purchase a new home.

"Oh, good morning," I say as I open the door to find Jack on the other side.

"Good morning," he says as he reaches for the back of his neck to rub it. "I wanted to apologize about last night and well, all of my behavior since you've arrived."

"Jack, that's already water under the bridge. You have nothing to apologize about."

"Yeah, I do. My parents raised me better. I've been acting like a horny teenager with no home training.

"I like you. A lot. I'm not sure what your plans are for Spring Valley, but I'd like to get to know you better either way.

"Maybe I can come see you wherever you land. Or we can FaceTime date or whatever it is these kids are doing to court long distance."

"I don't know, Jack. I had wanted to have this conversation yesterday before my interview, but you were gone. Now—"

"That's my fault. I took off to go fishing and clear my head. I haven't been drawn to anyone the way I'm drawn to you in years. I'm old and out of practice. I needed the time to sort through my feelings," he jumps in to say.

I sigh. "I like you too. I would like to get to know more about you, but … I'd rather not make this decision based on a romantic connection."

"I'm not asking you to decide on anything on account of me. Like I said, we can still get to know each other if Spring Valley doesn't work out for you. How about this?

"You need to get to know the town if you're going to stick around and I've lived here all my life. Allow me to take you on a Spring Valley tour. During that time, we can begin to get to know each other."

I chew on my lip as I look up into his eyes. He's adorable in this moment. I can't help feeling this connection between us.

"Okay, I guess that couldn't hurt. I'm supposed to look at a few listings today. We can go on the tour before that?"

"Yes, yes, would you like to come down for breakfast with me before we head out?"

"Oh, I was going to try to catch up with Jo."

"She's already downstairs with my boys. Those three are becoming partners in crime," he chuckles.

"In that case lead the way," I say with a smile.

I step out of my room and pull the door closed behind me. Jack places a hand on the small of my back but quickly removes it. I look up at him to find a blush on his cheeks.

"Well, Jack. If you're interested in getting to know me. You should know, touch is one of my love languages too. I don't mind."

"I'll keep that in mind. For now, I think it's best if I keep my hands to myself."

"Okay." I reach for his hand and lace my fingers through his. "Is this all right with you?"

He gives my fingers a gentle squeeze. The sparks that float up my arm bring a smile to my face. There's definitely chemistry here.

Jack

I almost gave up after Coral didn't come down for dinner last night and Lauren informed me Coral had ordered dinner up to her room. Courtland has always known how to get under my skin.

I wouldn't put it pass him to only be showing interest in Coral because rumors got out that she has caught my attention. I still wish I knew what him and Lisa fought about to make her not speak to him ever again before her death. However, I'm not going to allow any of that to get to me today.

"The ride to main street is so breathtaking it goes by faster than you know. I truly didn't think you were that far from the library yesterday. I had planned to walk back," Coral says into the silence of my truck.

I scoff. "You never would have made it. Not in those shoes you had on last night."

She releases a beautiful laugh. "Yeah, Courtland warned me and offered me a ride."

I stiffen a bit at the mention of the one person I don't want to think about. Working my jaw, I try to swallow down my anger. Breakfast went well with the kids, and we've been having a good time so far.

"I sorry to bring him up. Listen, I don't want to bring any drama. I only accepted the ride after he told me a lovely story about how your wife tried to make the same walk and you came to her rescue."

I sigh. "Courtland wasn't always such an asshole. Lisa adored him up until they fell out. She's probably rolling in her grave to see what he's been up to now."

"Family can be rough. My nieces thought their father would step in after my sister's death. I gave him every opportunity to be there for them, he just never stepped up."

"You've done such an amazing job with Jo. I would love to meet your other girls."

"Thank you. Your boys are sweet. You just might get to meet my others as well.

"I plan to buy a house they will feel welcome to come to. They're supposed to be on their way back home soon. If things come together, I'm sure you'll get the opportunity."

"If you decide to stay, Spring Valley has a whole lot to offer once you get to know it."

"It's already growing on me."

"Do you like to cook?"

"Yes, but my JC is the kitchen connoisseur."

"Well, our first stop will be Harry's farm. You live in Spring Valley, you should know Harry. Most of the town gets their fresh produces from his place. You'll love it here," I say as I pull up to Harry's farm.

I climb out of the truck and look down at my watch before I round the pickup to open the door for Coral. Holding my hand out, I wait for her to place her small one in mine. The moment she does the hum is there.

Every time our skin touches I feel alive again. I drop my gaze to her lips but remind myself that I don't have the freedom to go kissing those soft pillows. No matter how much I want to.

I clear my throat. "You're probably tired of burgers and beer. How about we get some produce and make something else for dinner later," I say.

"That sounds promising. I don't see why not."

This time I do place my hand on the small of her back as we make our way into the barn where Harry sets up to sell to the public. There's such a sense of comfort between us. Now that I'm not overthinking things, I'm able to enjoy being in the company of this gorgeous woman.

"How did the interview go? Do you like our library?"

"I love it. Flo is a hoot. She pretty much offered me the job on the spot."

"Do you mind if I ask what will make your final decision?"

"Finding a home. I don't just want a house; I want someplace that will feel like home. Although I'm looking for space for my girls to come visit anytime they want, in reality this will be my first time ever living on my own.

"So I also need to feel safe. I'm hoping I can find that before I give my final decision."

"And Cash is helping you?"

"Yeah, he and Flo felt he would be the best fit for me."

"Would you mind if I helped out with that? I have someplace I think would be perfect for you."

"Not at all. I'm open to any suggestions. It only takes one. I'll know it's home from the time I walk in."

"I'll let Cash know. He can add it to his list."

"Um, now I'm curious, Jack Harrington."

I give her a wink. "I'm hoping you stay. I'm pulling out all the stops to show you Spring Valley at its best."

"We shall see. We shall see."

CHAPTER NINE

Home Sweet Home

Coral

I had a wonderful time with Jack today. Spring Valley truly is an amazing little town. It has all the staples of the perfect small town.

Everyone I've met so far has been sweet and welcoming. Jack seems to know everyone by name. I can't say I didn't notice how everyone seems to love him.

I fell in love with the little candle shop and spent so much time in the bookstore, Mayor Cash had to come meet me in town for our appointment.

Jack needed to head back to the B&B for lunch service, and he mentioned something about new guests arriving and wanting to get things ready for them. I was a little disappointed to see him go. However, he did leave me with a belly full of butterflies when he tugged me in to peck my lips before placing a lingering kiss on my forehead before saying goodbye.

"I can already see you don't like this one either," Mayor Cash says as we stand in the foyer of the third property he's shown me.

"I mean, it's nice. They all have been, but they don't feel like home," he says the last part with me.

"I hear you. I know just what you mean. I have one more to show you today. I might have to expand the search to a town or two over."

"Oh, I was hoping to stay in Spring Valley. Especially since I love to spend so much time at the library. I don't want to have to rush to leave during the winter months."

"I think you might like this last one. I wasn't expecting to show it although I know how perfect it will be. It's a private listing," he says.

"Would this be the one your uncle mentioned?"

"Yes, ma'am. Come on, this one will speak for itself."

We turn to leave this house without going any farther. I don't want to waste his time looking around a place I have no interest in. We climb back into his truck and take off.

A smile comes to my face as I read a text from Jo. I think the town is growing on her too. I truly hope this next house is the one.

My brows begin to wrinkle as we're heading in what looks to be the direction of the B&B. The thought of finding a home this close to Jack makes my heart race. I don't know how to feel about it.

To be honest, I have a mix of emotions. On one hand, it would be nice to have Jack and his boys close by if I ever need a hand. However, on the other hand, there's a little pressure knowing a man I could potentially date lives so nearby. What if things don't work out?

When Cash makes a left in the opposite direction from the B&B I relax a bit. The grounds leading to the property are nicely kept. I can't help wondering how much of the land comes with the house.

"This property sits on twenty acres of land, but the house itself comes with two acres. The house has six bedrooms five and a half baths. It used to be serviced by it's own well separate from the towns water system, but the owner had the plumbing routed to the city line about six months ago.

"The house was completed a year ago. So it's considered new construction. It pretty much checks off your checklist. I would have brought you here first, but I know the sentimental value it has to the owner. I thought you might like something else before getting to this one."

I take a moment to think over his words. Jack called him to suggest this one for me. I get the feeling he's somehow connected to this property.

I gasp. "Is Jack the owner?"

"Yes, ma'am. He owns the land. This was a gift for Aunt Lisa before she got sick. She fell ill before Uncle Jack could finish it.

"To be honest, I never thought he would finish it. The guys had been trying to get him to sell but he's been adamant about not putting it on the market. Chance and Hershel ride over to maintain the place once a week."

"Why is he allowing you to show it to me?"

"Miss Coral, you have no idea how much you've affected my uncle in the short time you've been here. I get the feeling he wants you to stick around and no matter if you're dating him or not, he wants you close enough for him and the guys to keep an eye on you. It's just the way we're built." He shrugs.

I furrow my brows. I don't know how to feel about this. Clearly, the home is important to him.

"I know this all might seem like a lot, but I think you're going to love the house once you get inside," he says as he pulls to a stop in front of a gorgeous two-story home.

We both step out of the car. I stand speechless as I look at the home and the appealing front. The house is a gray color that has a hint of blue in it. The rooftop has blue shingles, and the shutters are a rich navy color.

There's an adorable porch swing. Then there are two rocking chairs with a table set between them. The flowerpots at the bases of the windows add so much charm.

This home feels like it was made with love. The front door is so inviting with its pretty glass and navy-blue frame. Cash opens it and steps back to allow me entry.

When I step into the foyer, my breath is taken away. This was not what I was expecting. The open airiness, the stunning chandeliers it's all a mix of modern vibes meets country chic. It speaks of my life past, present, and the future I envision.

"Over here is the den. It was the first space I thought of when you mentioned your book club with your daughter and nieces. You could even get some of the ladies from town to join and you'd have plenty of room."

"This is so gorgeous. I could only hope to recreate this look with new furniture."

"Miss Coral, all the furnishings are included. You're welcome to put your own items in but you don't have to. All Uncle Jack asks is that you let him know when you want to change something out so he can help and have a chance to store anything he doesn't want to see trashed," Cash says.

"I wouldn't touch a thing."

"He did say to let you know that you could. Don't be afraid to make it your home."

"How much is the asking price?"

"That he wants to tell you himself. Would you like to see the kitchen? It's a chef's dream."

"I, uh, I don't think I want to see anymore."

"Good, you want to talk to Uncle Jack and then I'll write up the contract?"

"No, I'm going to think about the others and see if there's a way I could make them feel like home."

"But why? I've been in the real estate business for a long time. I always know when someone has found their home. It's in your eyes. You love this one.

"It has everything you asked me for and more. There's even a firepit out back. Perfect for you and your girls to sit, talk, and make new memories."

"You said it yourself, you were hoping I would fall in love with one of the other homes so your uncle wouldn't have to part with this place. This was a labor of love, I … I just can't."

"Maybe I said too much. I know what I thought before we got here but seeing you here. Knowing you appreciate the place for what it is, I think it was always meant to be your home.

"The fact that it means so much to Uncle Jack and he asked me to show it says a whole lot about so much. Listen, talk to my uncle before you make any decisions. That sparkle in your eyes says you'll love and care for this home the way it deserves. I think that's all he wants," he says.

"It's a lot to think about. For now, let's head back. I'll talk to Jack and if this sits well tomorrow, I'll come back and have a walk through with Jo."

Jack

"How did it go?" I ask as Coral and Cash walk through the door.

I haven't been able to get Coral off my mind since I left her this afternoon when Cash met us in town to take her house hunting. Many won't understand why or how I could be willing to allow her to walk the house I started building with my late wife.

I blurted the offer out this morning without thinking much about it. However, I've had time to think about it since, and it still feels right. What's not right is how I forgot what Lisa asked of me.

That house shouldn't have sat vacant for so long or maybe it should have. It's been waiting for the right owner. Someone to love the heart and soul put into it.

"She loved Willowbrook."

"Is that the last one?"

"Yes, ma'am. Willowbrook Lane."

"Good to hear. You want to come to my office and talk? I can hand you the keys if you decide you're staying."

"Jack, I do think we need to talk. I love the house, but I don't think I can put in an offer. It means so much to you."

I sigh. "Come, let's take a walk instead. It seems this talk will get a little deeper than I planned."

I pick up the Walkie Talkie to get Chance to come man the desk. He lets me know he's on his way. However, instead of coming alone, he shows up with Jo at his side.

"We got it, Pop. You go on," Chance says.

"I'll leave you two to it. If you guys need me for anything let me know, I'll be happy to help. I'm not looking for a commission or anything. Uncle Jack you already know I'll write it all up as a private sale between the two of you."

"Sale? What you selling, Pop?"

I heave a heavy breath. "Coral might purchase Willowbrook."

"Are you serious? You're going to let it go? I didn't think you would ever—"

"We can talk about it later, son."

"Are we hurting for cash? What aren't you telling me?"

I roll my eyes. "No, we're not hurting for cash. This has nothing to do with the money. I will talk to you later."

"It's a beautiful home, Miss Marks. Jo, you would be really close when you come to visit your mama."

I shake my head and move to place a hand on the small of Coral's back to lead her out the front door. Once outside, I start for the path that wraps the house to head for the brewery. We walk in silence for a beat.

"Jack, I—"

"Lisa wanted me to sell. She asked me to make sure it went to the right owner. Today, I realized just how much I ignored or blocked out in my grief.

"We had long talks I put out of my mind for so long. Things I've questioned since she's been gone but already have the answer to from her lips. My grief was so deep, I only saw it, not the way out."

"Do you see your way out now?"

"I think I do. At least I'm starting to. I don't think I was allowing myself to because I felt like I failed her.

"I could have done more, I should have done more. That's what I've been telling myself for the last year. If only I had found better doctors or surrounded her with more love."

"Jack, I can't tell you how to feel or say that I know how you feel, but I can tell you that I had a lot of the same thoughts about my sister. I wanted to bring her back for her girls, I wanted her back with me.

"I blamed myself for so many things that I had no control over. At some point it clicked that I was doing my best which is all she would ever ask of me," she says and laces her fingers with mine.

I give her hand a gentle squeeze. "It took a while, but I think I'm starting to get there. Lisa had been preparing me to live without her. Long before she died, she had been getting me ready, I see that so much more clearly."

"Did your fishing trip help with that?"

"Yeah, in a way it did. Terry, that's my best friend. He lost his wife too. He got me to thinking and a lot came to the surface," I reply.

"Like the house?"

I nod. "For a year she was in nothing but pain. When she was lucid, she tried to prepare me.

"I would shut down every time. I didn't want to hear any of it. In my mind, we just needed to keep fighting.

"She was going to get better. She would beat that thing for me and the boys. I was determined to finish the house for when she did.

"We designed that place before she fell ill. I had just started the build when she went in to the doctor about some pains she hadn't told me about. It was like from the day of that visit everything fell apart.

"I've been alone and stewing in my own shit for some time now, but today I remembered the talk we had about that house. Lisa wanted it filled with life. She wanted someone who would appreciate it to live there and breathe life into it," I explain.

"But why me? Can you help me to understand why now and why me?"

"I think she would have wanted it to be you. A fresh start for a fresh start. It's something she used to tell the boys all the time.

"First day of school they had to have a fresh haircut and new shoes. New team to play on, they got all new gear. I think she would want you to have a new home for your new journey.

"Plenty of folks have made offers, but none of them felt right. I always got the feeling they wanted the land more than the house. It would have been the two acres then an offer for more until none of my family's land has my name on it. That wasn't why we built it in the first place."

"Do you mind if I ask why you did?"

"We wanted to redo our rooms at the B&B and move over to Willowbrook to have more available space for guests at the inn. Things had been picking up, and Lisa was a big advocate of bringing life back into town."

"I feel like there's something you're not saying," she says softly as we take a seat on the bench outside the brewery.

I used to sit right here to think and dream as a young man. I dreamed up the perfect life for me, Lisa, and my boys right here. Back then nothing was impossible.

I sigh. "The tension between me and Courtland. It's over a lot more than his sister. Courtland has been trying to get us all in town to sell off parts of our land to some developers.

"Lisa hated the idea. She was one of the leaders in the community doing all she could to keep the town thriving. Fundraisers, creating tourist attractions, getting the boys to help her with social media to get the word out.

"She was the best at it. No one has taken the reins or been able to do what she used to. We're not getting new blood, and some are starting to cave.

"My friend Terry and I have the most land left. Others have sold, moved on or passed on and their land has been sold off. As the mayor, Cash has been trying to stop it all from happening and put a lid on his daddy before it's too late.

"However, if they keep acquiring the small pieces bit by bit, Terry and I won't matter. Spring Valley as we know it will be lost. I just get frustrated thinking about it. I feel like I'm failing Lisa again.

"The library meant a lot to her. She and Flo did a lot of fundraising together. I guess I have a few reasons to want you to stay. Maybe having you around will help Flo get back into the swing of things." I shrug.

"Can I think about the house?"

"I hope you do think about the house. Give it as much thought as you need. It's not going anywhere," I say.

"As far as the fundraising, I would love to help. That sort of used to be my thing. Me and my girls are like event ninjas.

"That's one of the things that caused me and my ex to grow apart. When he was ready to start thinking about slowing down and taking more time for ourselves, I couldn't let down all the people who benefited from the time I gave.

"I don't consider myself too old to do good. My ex was ready to reward himself for all he did give over the years. I can't blame him.

"I don't even fault him. Two things can be true at once. I just know I'm not done. I'd love to hear more about the things done in the past to see if I can spark them anew," she says with that smile on her face.

"All the more reason for you to stay," I say with a smile.

"I still don't know the asking price."

"You wouldn't take it as a gift, would you?"

"*Jack*," she drags out.

"Fine, I knew you would say that." I chuckle. "One fifty, fully furnished and all."

"Oh my God, you have to be kidding me. It's twice the size of the other options. The largest of the other three I saw was five fifty. Your place has to appraise for at least a million if not more," she gasps.

"One fifty, Coral. I won't ask you for a dime more. All I ask is that you don't go selling to those damn developers when they come knocking."

"What about after I'm gone?"

I swallow hard not wanting to think about that but not wanting to repeat my mistakes either. "I hope that's not for a long time to come. Leave it to Jo. I get the feeling this is going to be home to her as much as it will be for you."

CHAPTER TEN

Crushed

Coral

"All of this was amazing. Your wife left some huge shoes to fill. I can see why no one else stepped up," I say as I flip through the albums Jack pulled out of some of the past fundraisers and events.

"I think all the town needs is the right person to take interest."

"This is true," I say and smile.

Over the past few days, I've been spending a lot of time getting to know more about Spring Valley and the community they have here. Jack has been very instrumental in that.

He has taken me to dinner in town almost every night. Our dates have been sweet and entertaining. I had a ball bowling with him, the mayor, and Emma last night.

Jo had planned to join us, but she received a call and changed her plans last minute. I'm not sure what that was about and I haven't seen her this morning to try to get answers.

She has been spending a lot of time with Chance and Hershel, but I still don't think she gets that they're both interested in her. However, I have noticed she hasn't been with either of them today. That reminds me that I need to call Mel and JC to see how they're doing and if they're on their way back anytime soon.

I don't know when I plan to go back home. When I do head back it will be to pack and settle my affairs. Spring Valley feels like home. Something I haven't felt in a very long time.

"Jo, Jo, is everything all right?" I heard Chance call with concern in his voice.

"No," Jo sobs, causing me to stand and rush to see what's going on.

"Jodie, what's going on, sweetheart?"

"Mom," she sobs and comes to wrap her arms around me. "I feel so stupid. I thought he loved me. I was going to introduce him to you when we got back home. I'm such an idiot. He's been cheating on me this whole time.

"I didn't want to believe it, but Marty sent me video proof and when I called to confront him, he didn't even deny it. It's like I meant nothing to him," she cries.

I stand confused. I didn't even know she was seeing anyone. I glance at Chance to find a furious expression on his face. Hershel has appeared and he looks as stunned as I feel.

"Honey, I didn't know you were seeing anyone," I whisper.

"You and daddy were going through the divorce. Mel and JC were going on their trip. It didn't feel like the time was right to introduce him or make everything about who I was seeing. I mean, you know JC left with Mel because of her breakup.

"I totally stayed behind to support you, but that jerk had a lot to do with why I didn't join them. Mel warned me about him. I should have listened to her."

"Hey, Jo-jo Bell, I can't say I take too kindly to hearing you in tears. You come on with me, I have the prefect thing for a broken heart," Jack croons as he comes to rub her back.

I can't help but smile. He's been calling her Jo-jo Bell for the last two days. I can tell he's become fond of her.

"Can Mom come too?"

"Of course, darlin'. Anyone who needs to mend a broken heart or just needs to be there for a loved one can join us. Nothing like friends and family to see you through," he says and winks.

I get the feeling he's talking to his boys. Jo having a boyfriend sort of changes a lot, I'm sure. Even if the asshole just broke her heart.

"Thanks, Jack. This means a lot. I thought he loved me.

"I had been planning our wedding in my head right here in Spring Valley. We had been talking about moving in together since my lease will be up soon," Jo says sadly.

"But now you can follow your heart," Chance says knowingly.

"Yeah. I don't know. I feel like telling you all of that might have jinxed my future."

"Or maybe telling me put it out there for the universe to pull it all in to you."

Jo gives a small smile. "I'd like to see it that way, but only time will tell."

Jo goes to link her arm through the arm Jack offers her. Me and the boys follow behind them, Chance and Hershel walking behind me.

"You knew she had a boyfriend?" I overhead Hershel hiss.

"Not until last night."

"Fuck. No wonder she hasn't been responding to either of our advances."

I stop and turn to face the two. "That may be, but Jo isn't going to get that you're interested until you come straight out and tell her. She's been missing your cues. She will keep you both in the friendzone if you don't move yourself out. Just some friendly advice."

"Yes, ma'am," they say in unison.

Jack

I'm spitting mad. I wish I could get my hands on the asshole who just broke Jo's heart. Her laughter has been like a bell of joy around here since she arrived.

I can see why my boys are smitten with her. Although Hershel looked like someone punched him in the gut and ripped out his heart when Jo said she had a boyfriend. I get the feeling Chance already knew from the expression on his face.

He looked exactly how I feel. I guess it's a good thing I never had girls. I don't know that I could say this would be my first reaction if Jo were my daughter.

However, I had to bite down my anger and do something helpful. So here we are. I brought Jo and the others out to the old theater behind the brewery house.

We don't use this place much anymore. There was a time we would have movie night once a month. Now, we don't have movie nights here and it's been a while since I've had the boys in here to mend one of their broken hearts.

"This place is awesome and oh my God, Jack this salted caramel milkshake is everything," Jo sings.

"Yeah, Pop. I can't believe I forgot about these. Totally going on the menu," Chance adds.

"Hey, Pop. Why'd we stop having movie nights? This place used to be packed."

"It was your mother's thing. I just haven't thought about bringing it back."

"Well, I think we should. I'm going to look into it. It would be nice to see this place packed out like it used to be."

"Yeah, Pop. It could mean another stream of revenue. I'm in," Hershel says.

"For now, let's get this popcorn going and the movie started."

"Thanks, Jack," Coral whispers.

"She's a good kid. She doesn't deserve this. The bastard doesn't know what he ruined."

"You sound like her father. He's going to be furious. No one is good enough for his baby."

"Can't blame him."

"Oh darn, I almost forgot," Jo groans as she looks down at her phone.

"What's up, honey?" Coral says.

"Uh, nothing. I need to go back to the inn for a second."

"Oh, for that thing?" Chance says.

"Yeah, for that."

"Oh, right. I'll come with you," Hershel says.

"You can start the movie. We'll be right back," Jo says.

I lift a brow as the three rush off. I look to Coral, and she looks as puzzled as I feel. However, now that we're alone, I can't help but crowd her space and cup the side of her face.

"I had a great time at dinner last night," I say as I look down into her eyes.

"I did too."

I run my thumb across her full bottom lip as I search her gaze. We've slowed things down a lot, but I've been dying to really kiss her again. I had gone in for a kiss last night, but it was interrupted.

"I only have one regret," I murmur.

"Is that so?" she breathes.

"Yes, it is, but I plan to make it right."

I lean in and capture her lips. She moans as she wraps her arms around my neck and lifts up on her toes. Grabbing a hold of her full ass, I pull her body into mine.

She runs her fingers though the back of my hair and sinks into me. I grow hard all over as her body softens against mine. I deepen the kiss and groan into her mouth.

"Wow, I thought you were lying. Go ahead, Mom. Get it."

Coral pulls away much too soon. I turn to find my boys, Jo, and two gorgeous young ladies staring back at us. Coral gasps and rushes into a group hug with the two newcomers.

"Oh, my babies. I'm so happy to see you two. What are you doing here?"

"Jo called and told us you might have found a place you like. We wanted to come see for ourselves," the taller of the two says.

"Okay, that might be why JC came back but I'm here to check out the guy Jo said you've been smooching with. Hello, Mister. I'm Mel, the favorite niece slash daughter," the other one says.

"Oh my God. Why do you girls insist on embarrassing me? Jack, Chance, Hershel these are my girls. This is JC and this is Mel. Mel, JC, this is Jack, Chance, and Hershel Harrington."

"Wow, did the women in your family drink from the goddess of beauty's personal cup," Hershel says.

"Well, aren't you sweet," Mel says.

"Did I say that out loud?" Hersh says as he blushes bright crimson.

"Yup, you did, handsome," Mel says.

"Please disregard my older sister. I'm pretty sure our mom dropped her a few times. We ignore her all the time. It works wonders."

"Girls, girls," Coral says as the two begin to bicker. "Oh, my. Where are you two going to stay? Jack, you said you guys are fully booked."

"We booked them in the last two rooms two days ago. Jo wanted to surprise you. We took care of everything," Chance says.

CHAPTER ELEVEN

Temper, Temper

Coral

"You didn't have to cancel your date because of us. I mean, that man is fine, fine. He's given zaddy vibes," Mel says as she lies across my bed.

It feels good to have all my girls here. After watching a movie with Jack and the boys, we all came up to my room to catch up. Jack needed to meet with Mayor Cash, so we canceled our lunch and made plans to meet up for a late dinner this evening.

"We didn't cancel because of you girls. His nephew needed to come talk to him," I say.

"Speaking of that man's relatives, what's up with his sons?" Mel croons.

"They're single but they're both younger than you. I know that's not your thing," Jo giggles.

"You're just saying that to keep them to yourself. I see you," Mel says and narrows her eyes at Jo who's sitting crossed legged at the top of the bed.

"I'm good on men for a while. Besides, Chance and Hershel are cool. I don't think either of them are interested in more than a friendship with me."

I look at Jo and purse my lips. I can't believe she still doesn't see how either young man sees her. My daughter is bright but when it comes to men, she can't seem to buy a clue.

"I don't know. I saw the way that one was looking at you," JC says.

"Which one?" Mel asks.

"The taller one. I think he's Chance," JC replies.

"Right, because the other one kept sneaking peeks our way. However, I don't think he was looking at me," Mel says.

JC rolls her eyes and flips her body over so she's now lying half on her sister. I sit in the accent chair in the corner smiling at my three.

"I'm with Jo. Men suck. I don't need another one anytime soon. I'm going to focus on me and my career."

"Too bad Ashton works with you," Mel says.

"Ugh, don't remind me. I still have two weeks before I need to be back in the office. I don't want to see his stupid face when I go back," JC whines and pouts.

"Well, I don't know what you're talking about," Jo says. "Chance has become a friend. I don't think he looks at me any way other than that."

"*Okay*," JC drags out. "If that's what you want to tell yourself. I never did like that Jarold guy anyway. Guys suck. All they do is play with your feelings and act like it was your fault."

"Uncle Ralph is a good one. How do you think he's going to take you dating, Mom?" Mel asks.

"I don't know how he will feel. We ended things on good terms. I think we both planned to move forward in whatever way would make us happy. I don't foresee any drama."

"Yeah, Dad isn't like that," Jo says.

"I don't know. When feelings get involved things change. That was Uncle Ralph's box for how many years?"

"Ew, that's still my dad. I don't want to hear that mess," Jo groans.

"What the hell?" JC gasps and sits up as something crashes downstairs.

"I don't know what that was," I say and jump up to rush to the door.

The girls are right on my heels as I rush down the stairs. I follow the voices into the dining room once I'm on the main floor. I find Jack and an angry looking Mayor Cash.

One of the tables has been turned over. It now lies upside down broken. Items that were probably once on top are now on the floor.

"Is everything all right?" I ask.

"No, my father is the world's biggest as—"

"Cash," Jack calls in warning as he nods toward the other entrance of the dining room.

Emma is standing there clutching a stuffed bear as she looks on with wide eyes. Mel snaps into action and goes to squat in front of Emma. Mel was once on the path to become a teacher before she changed course and ended up working for a local councilman back home. I'm not surprised she's the one to rush to Emma's side.

"Hi, cutie. My name is Mel. What's yours?"

"I'm Emma."

"And who do we have here?" Mel says pointing to Emma's bear.

"I just got him. Uncle Cash gave him to me before we came over. I haven't named him yet," Emma says.

"Do you mind if I call him Mr. Bear until you decide on his permanent name?"

Emma nods. Mel stands to her full height and holds her hand out to Emma. Emma looks to Cash then back at Mel's hand.

"I saw those rocking chairs out front. My Uncle Ralph told me bears like Mr. Bear love when you rock them in rocking chairs.

They love it even more when you tell them a story while you're rocking. How about I tell you and Mr. Bear a story while the grown ups clean up in here."

Emma takes her hand with a big smile on her face as she nods. I smile at my niece taking control in an awkward situation. Turning my attention back to Mayor Cash, I find him with a scowl on his face as his brow are drawn.

"Coral's nieces arrived this morning. That was Mel," Jack offers.

"What's going on?" I ask again.

"Mr. Jenkins broke his leg on his farm last week. His son and daughter think it's time to let the place go. My father is trying to purchase the land to back door them and sell to those bastard developers.

"Mr. Jenkins would never allow his land to be sold to those bastards. All my money is tied up so I can't make the purchase. I've been buying land to hold this all off as much as I can, but I'm going broke at this point.

"This town isn't what it used to be. If I can't figure out how to gain an influx of cash or bring some new life into Spring Valley, the whole town is fucked. I'm doing my best, I've been trying so hard, but Dad is hell-bent on ruining this town street by street," he bites out.

"How can we help?" JC asks.

"I was just about to ask the same thing. What can we do?" Jo says.

"JC works in marketing and social media management for a non-for-profit. They're always looking for a new cause to back. Mel works for a councilman, so she has plenty of resources.

"Spring Valley has so many unique experiences you can all capitalize off. Put us to work. Let's brainstorm and see if we can help out."

"How much time do you ladies have?" Cash sighs.

Jack

"Thank you. You have no idea how much this means to me," I say to Coral as we take a walk around the property.

"Me nor my girls were going to stand by and not step in somehow. I already had a ton of ideas that your photo albums sparked."

"You're all remarkable. I think things might turn around with all y'all came up with."

"JC's organization seems all in to hear more about the town. If they come on board, I know things will take a turn for the best but even without them this town really does have a lot to offer."

"That it does."

I can't blame Cash for the way he blew up when the call came in about Courtland and the sale. We were talking about the situation as it was.

Cash is a good kid. He's trying to do the right thing by the town and Lisa's memory. I had no idea until today that he promised Lisa he would save the town from Courtland.

I also hadn't known before today that he's been putting out his own money to protect the town. That was the last thing he told me before he got the call. Cash is wealthy from his mother's side of the family.

However, he's burning through his wealth to save the town and it ain't right. Coral and her girls have jumped right in to help out, and I think there may be a way to make this all right.

"This farm is so beautiful. Mel and Jo are right, there's so much this place can do to attract tourists and visitors. I know Spring Valley felt like home from the moment we pulled onto the property, it's only been growing on me since."

"Does that mean you're thinking of staying?"

"It does."

"And the house?"

"I'll take it. Although, I do have a counteroffer. Five fifty, not a cent less. I know that's still way off the mark, but it seems like a fair halfway point," she says.

"Um," I grunt. "Fine. I get to have you here so I'm not going to fight you too hard."

"Good, I don't want to have your funky vibes in my new home."

"Say what now?"

"I thought we could head to the house for dinner tonight. Hershel told me about a place that delivers. How about we go to the house, I can check out the rest of it, and we can have dinner there without any interruptions."

The thought of getting to have her all to myself kicks my old butt in gear. I move faster than I have in years. Getting us into my truck, I get us over to Willowbrook before anyone can catch us and stop us.

Coral releases that beautiful laugh all the way to the house from the passenger seat. I can't deny the pang in my chest as we pull up. I stopped coming by after Lisa's death.

It had been too painful. When I step out of the truck a light breeze passes by me, like a caress. I close my eyes and inhale deeply.

I'm doing the right thing. Lisa wanted me to sell this house to someone who would make it a home. She also told me to find happiness again.

I was up most of last night remembering her words. In this moment, I feel like Lisa is here pushing me to let go and be happy. No one can replace the years Lisa and I spent together but I can start fresh if I try.

"Oh, I'm sorry. Maybe we shouldn't have come here." Coral's soft voice pulls me from my musing.

"No, I'm fine. I'll get the key so we can go inside," I say and go up on the porch to retrieve the spare key.

"Is there anything special I should order?"

"No, I've had it all. I'll take whatever you order. Tell Tim I said to send over a bottle of wine and to put everything on my tab."

"Oh, I had planned to treat you tonight."

"Now, I've budged once tonight. I don't think I have it in me to concede again this evening, darlin'."

She releases a chuckle. "Fine. I'll be quick so we can take the tour."

I nod and point toward the living room. "I'm going to turn on some music."

I'd be lying if I said my nerves weren't starting to comeback. I move into the living area go to open the record player, then begin to go through the records. Lisa and I had eclectic taste in music.

Terry and Marly gave us a lot of these records to make sure we had some of their favorites when we would get together. My palms get a little sweaty as I dig through looking for the right tunes.

"Hey you," Coral sings as she walks up behind me and wraps her arms around my waist. I turn slightly to look back at her. "They said our food will be here in thirty minutes. What should we do until then?"

"If I can find the right music, I plan to ask you to dance with me."

"Well, let me see what you've got. I love records."

I step out of the way and allow her to dig through the crates here. I can't help taking her in and looking her over. She looks gorgeous.

The burgundy sundress she has on flows over her body showing off her curves while floating around her legs. Her ass looks great in it. She shifts a little and her ass jiggles beneath the fabric.

"Luther, Teddy, Freddie, Barry, oh you have all the greats in here. Who you been hanging with, Mr. Harrington?"

"That would be Terry and Marly. My best friend and his late wife."

She looks back at me. It's clear to see the empathy in her eyes. I give her a smile and peck her lips.

"I have lived a life. There have been good times and bad ones. I have my memories and luckily, I still have Terry when I need him."

"Jack, I don't want to move too fast if you're not ready."

"Hold on, I think I know just the song."

We switch places and I reach for the "Rock Me Tonight" album. Soon Freddie Jackson is crooning "You are My Lady." I pull Coral into me and begin to sway her around the room.

"I'm moving at the pace that feels right. This feels right. Every time I have you in my arms, whenever we're together," I say.

She smiles up at me as she begins to play with the hairs at the nape of my neck. We lock eyes and get lost in the music. I don't know how long we've been dancing when the doorbell rings and breaks the trance we're in.

Coral clears her throat and goes to answer the door. I watch her walk away and need to adjust myself as I do. I look up at the ceiling as I try to send up a prayer that I don't mess this up tonight.

"Jack, where would you like to eat?"

"We can sit at the dining table or the kitchen island, either works for me," I call back.

"The kitchen island seems more intimate. Is that all right?"

"It's perfect, darlin'," I say and begin to walk toward her voice.

CHAPTER TWELVE

Still Got It

Jack

I take a sip off wine and work my mouth to clean the food out of my teeth. The food and conversation have been nice, but the sexual tension between us has me hot under the collar. I take another sip of wine as I roam my gaze over Coral.

"That was delicious. Do you want to give me that tour now?"

"What rooms have you been through? Where should we start?"

"I didn't get very far. I was charmed by the curb appeal. Then I knew I was in love with the place from the foyer. After that I saw the den and was sold."

"So you haven't seen much at all."

"Nope, I still haven't seen the master bedroom."

"Is that where you want to start or end?"

"Ball's in your court, Jack. I'm following your lead."

I grasp the back of her neck and lean in to capture her lips. Her mouth is extra sweet from dinner. As our tongues dance together, I can't help but groan.

I've wanted this woman from the time I looked into her eyes. Needing to get closer to her, I stand from my seat, knocking the island stool over with the movement. Coral hops down from her seat and I wrap my arms around her, lifting her into me.

She moans into my mouth as I deepen the kiss. Coaxing her legs around my waist, I then start for the master bedroom. Although she is hesitant to lock around me. I tighten my hold as I go.

"I've got you," I groan into her mouth.

"Are you sure you're okay? You don't have to carry me," she pants.

"I'm old, woman. Not weak. I've been working this farm since I was a boy. I'm fine."

She chuckles and begins to kiss all over my face. I can't help but laugh with her. Only this woman would know just how to take the nerves out of the situation.

Stepping into the bedroom, I then place her back on her feet. I look down at her and bite my lip as her nipples strain against the thin fabric of her sundress. Lifting my hands, I brush the backs of my fingertips from the straps of her dress down to her wrists.

"You're so beautiful. It's like a light shines from within you," I murmur.

"Can I be honest with you?"

"I'm going to take a chance and say yes."

She laughs. "You're handsome, Jack. Very attractive. That's not what I was going to comment on.

"What I was going to say is that it's been so long since I've been with a man. Even longer since I've been with one other than my ex-husband. I'm a little nervous."

"It's been a long time for me too, but I think I remember a thing or two. If it's terrible, let me know. I take instructions well."

"Something tells me you'll be fine on your own. I'm just not sure how beautiful you'll think I am without the clothes. Things look a lot different from my college years."

"I'm sporting a dad bod. Far from my football days. Not that I would dare judge the body of a woman offering me hers."

"We'll see—"

Before she can finish her words, I move in and crush my lips to hers. The kiss is hot and heavy. When she reaches for the buttons of my shirt, I take over and release the top few buttons before pulling the shirt over my head.

Coral reaches to plant her hands on my torso and begins to snicker. I lift a brow at her as I watch her run her hands over the gray hair on my chest.

"Jack this is not a dad bod. You're very sexy for a man who's fifty-one."

I snort. "If you say so. Come here, darlin', let me get you out of that dress."

Instead of letting me undress her, she reaches for my belt to release it. She then unfastens and unzips my jeans. I don't realize I'm holding my breath until I spring free from my pants as she shoves them down my hips.

The gasp that leaves her lips makes me smile. The more she looks me over, the more confidence I gain. I can relate to her nerves and apprehension from being with someone outside of my wife for the first time in so long.

"Well damn, Jack. I wasn't expecting any of this," she says and bites her lip.

I reach for her and push the straps of her dress from her shoulders. The fabric floats down to the floor into a pool at her feet. She's left standing in a little pair of panties. Her breasts are full and turn up with the perfect little brown nipples.

Her belly isn't as firm as I'm sure it once was, but I love it. It's a sign I'm dealing with a real woman. The way her mound looks like it's resting on her upper thighs—almost as if on display on a pedestal—it's a total turn on.

She begins to squirm and fidget, crossing her arms over her breasts. I shake my head and close the gap between us. Gently, I pull her arms around my neck, then wrap my arms around her, and palm her plush ass.

She lifts on her toes as I dip my head to take her lips. Coral moans in my mouth as I begin to knead her ass and really get into the kiss. Her small hands gliding over my back feel amazing.

"Jack," she cries out as I pinch her nipple and begin to kiss my way down her neck.

I get to her breast and suck her other nipple into my mouth. She begins to dig her nails into my ass, trying to get closer to me. I lift her in my arms once again.

A yelp leaves her lips as she clings to me. I chuckle as I walk her over to the bed and place her on the side. When I pull away, she looks up at me with so much lust in her eyes.

Lowering to my knees slowly, I then peel her panties away. Tossing them over my shoulder, I then hook her legs over my shoulders. I feel the moment we both push all the worries and concerns to the backs of our minds. I'm just a man and she's a beautiful woman I want badly.

I lick my lips as I stare at her pretty pussy. Her sexy lips are already glistening for me. I groan as I run my thumb through them, then dive in.

"Oh shit, Jack," she cries as she bows off the bed.

I hum into her pussy as I find my rhythm. Grasping her hips, I keep her from running from me. I haven't lost my touch when it comes to eating pussy.

She's crying my name and tugging at my hair in no time. The deeper I push in, the louder she gets. I can't help the grin that comes to my lips.

"You taste so good, baby girl," I groan as I back off to use my fingers to bring her pleasure.

I reach for my length with my free hand. I give a few strokes, but I really want to be inside her. When her body begins to quake, I know I'm not going to be able to wait much longer.

I lift to my feet as I stick my fingers into my mouth and hum around them. Coral locks eyes with me and gives me a heated stare. My chest fills with pride to have a woman look back at me with such desire.

It's a reminder that I'm still a man and I can still bring my partner pleasure. I grab one of her legs and open her up to me as I grab my shaft to guide my way into her wet center.

"Oh yeah," I groan as I sink into her snug heat.

I plant one of my feet on the mattress and begin to thrust down into her. My eyes roll back, and I toss my head back as the feeling of being inside her courses through me.

"Shit, you feel so good."

The sound of her wet pussy and her moans is driving me crazy. I drop my head back down and fix my gaze on her perfect tits bouncing. I groan wanting to taste her skin and the light sheen of sweat that's beginning to dew. Grasping her waist, I keep pulling her toward me as I rock into her.

Her walls suck, ripple, and tighten around me. The way she's throwing it back at me is taking me for a loop. It's like we've found a way to move in sync as if this isn't our first time together.

I know one thing for sure, this won't be the last. If I wanted this woman before, I know I will crave her from this day forward. I pull out, not wanting it to end. I go to roll her on her side so I can climb on the bed behind her, but she surprises me when she pushes me onto my back and moves to straddle me.

"I love a good ride," she purrs against my lips.

"It's all yours," I say with a smile on my face as I hold my length up for her to seat herself.

I groan as she slides down on me and begins to circle her hips. Then she begins to bounce and rock on top of me like I'm a prized bull. I grab ahold of her hips as it's all I can do to stay in control of my own body.

My toes curl and I start to sweat profusely. Her pussy is dripping down my balls and into the crack of my ass. She so wet and her skin is so soft.

I lift up and pull one of her nipples into my mouth to suck on it while she rides me. I groan as she getting increasingly wet and starts to moan and keen loudly.

"Oh fuck, that turns you on, darlin'. What else do you like?"

"Your dick is so hard and thick. Keep sucking and fuck me back. I love a dominate partner who knows how to work my body," she pants while circling her hips as she rocks her pussy against me with the motion.

"You don't have to ask me twice."

I begin to thrust up into her as I hold her hips steady. I think we both lose our minds with the motion. When I feel her come around me, I flip her onto her back and pin her legs back.

I shift my legs until I have them beneath her. Her ass and pussy are tilted up into the air. Angling my hips, I start to pound into her.

"Oh my God, Jack. Yes, that's it right there. Dear God, you know how to fuck. Yes, yes, don't stop, please."

I groan and slap her ass. I haven't fucked like this in years. Not even with Lisa. I feel ten years younger and energized. My eyes begin to cross when I feel her walls pulse against me as if she's squeezing them to.

"Coral, baby girl. I'm going to come if you keep doing that."

She releases a breathy laugh and does it again. I smile and grab her throat as I lean in to kiss her while still pumping my hips. It's when she sucks my tongue into her mouth and begins that squeezing again that I lose control and begin to release into her hot, tight pussy.

"Fuck," I growl into her mouth.

"I'd say you still got it," she pants beneath me.

We both begin to laugh breathlessly. I roll onto my back and look up at the ceiling. That was amazing.

CHAPTER THIRTEEN

Miss Please

Coral

Wow, I wasn't expecting last night. Jack shocked the heck out of me. The sex was amazing, and it didn't hurt that he put in multiple rounds. I thought I might get two maybe three out of him.

Ralph and I had slowed down to one or two a night before we just stopped having sex at all. Jack had no problem reaching for me throughout the night. He also wasn't put off when I woke him with a little gift early this morning.

The man has a lot to offer, and I wanted to explore all that was on the menu. The fact that we could banter and laugh during our love making was refreshing. It took the nerves and tension out of the evening.

I smile to myself as I feel his lips on my bare shoulder when I wake. The sun is shining into the room, and I can smell coffee in the air. My body aches in places it hasn't ached in a very long time.

"I'm not ready to get out of bed," I murmur.

"I figured you were going to say that. I would love to lie here with you all day, but I need to get back to the inn. I have a shipment of yeast, honey, hops, and barrels coming in for the brewery.

"I can't always trust those boys to receive shipments. Hershel will argue the price and Chance will accept and sign without going through to check things. I made you breakfast, I just didn't want to leave without saying anything," Jack says into my ear then nuzzles my neck.

"Oh, I'm sorry. I don't want to hold up your day. I'll get Jo or one of the other girls to come back for me. I know they all will want to see the house."

"I was going to leave the truck here for you. Chance is already heading over to pick me up."

I groan. "I'm too old for the walk of shame."

"Ain't nothing to be ashamed about. We're two consenting adults and we had one passionate night. The first of many more I hope."

I turn to look over my shoulder and find him staring at me heatedly. Oh, there will be plenty more if I can help it. The way this man showed out last night was enough to make me change all my plans if I hadn't already decided to move here to Spring Valley.

"Yes, it was the first of many more. Thank you for breakfast and leaving the truck."

He pecks my lips and then my nose. I close my eyes as he goes to kiss my forehead. I can't help the smile that comes to my face.

"You take all the time you need. Look around, make yourself comfortable with your new place. I'll see you at the inn when you return."

"See you soon."

I watch as he stands and whistles his way out of the room. I begin to make a mental list of all the things I need to do over the next few days before I head out to pack my old home and have everything moved here to Spring Valley.

Once the move is final, I can dive into the planning and execution of *Operation Save The Town*. There's so much to do. As much as I would love to lie in bed, I should get moving myself to begin to get things rolling.

With a sigh, I get up and head into the bathroom for a shower. A smile comes to my face as I remember Jack getting up after each round to get a cloth to clean my sex before climbing into bed to cuddle with me. It was the little things that made last night special for me.

I begin to sing to myself as the hot water cascades down on my skin. Being in Spring Valley while staying at the B&B has felt right. However, being here in this house feels like home.

Having my plans set in my mind, I hop out of the shower and realize I have nothing to wear. Stepping into the room, I go to look for the dress I had on last night. When I enter the bedroom, I hear voices in the house. I tighten my towel around me and begin to look for something as a weapon.

"She's in the shower, I'm going to place the clothes on the bed for her," Mel calls through the house causing me to relax.

I put down the poker I grabbed from by the fireplace just as Mel steps into the room. However, not before this girl sees me with it and bursts into laughter.

Jo and JC come rushing in behind her. I palm my forehead and sigh. This might be worse than a walk of shame.

"Mom, what were you going to do with that?" Mel asks through her laughter.

My nieces have been calling me mom instead of aunty since a year after they lost their mother. It warms my heart every time. Our bond has grown so strong.

We were already close when my sister was alive. I have always been grateful that I could be there for them. As I look at them now, I can't help but think of how proud my sister would be.

"I'm taking the room across the hall with all the windows," Jo calls out as she dances her way into the room.

"Girl, you can have it. When I come to visit it will be for peace of mind. Do you see that bed? Mr. Jack was in here putting in work. I don't want to hear that," JC says.

"Ew, never mind," Jo murmurs.

"I'll take it. Don't none of that bother me. I still remember walking in on Uncle Ralph humping Mom. I cool backed right out and went on to mind my business," Mel says.

"What?" I gasp.

She waves me off. "All I saw was his sweaty ass and back. I covered my eyes and backed out the room. No big deal."

"I want to check out the other rooms upstairs," Jo says.

"Okay, cool. I brought you something to wear, Mom. By the way, this house is *nice*," Mel says dragging the last part out.

"All of you out. Let me get dressed and I'll walk the house with y'all. Then each of you can claim a room and I'll take notes of things you want moved out," I say.

"Huh?" JC says and frowns.

"Jack is leaving the place furnished. However, the things here have sentimental value to him. He'd like for me to give him a chance to store anything we might move."

"I'd just box all his shit up and give it to him then," JC mutters.

"Damn, JC," Mel and Jo say in unison.

"What? Tell me you weren't thinking the same thing."

"Yeah, maybe, but you didn't have to say it out loud," Jo says.

"I swear, I don't know how you work in your industry. Don't y'all have to be people friendly?" Mel says.

"Whatever. Get dressed, Mom. I have a few things I want to go to town for, and I'd like to see it for myself."

"Hershel offered to take you and show you around," Jo says.

JC rolls her eyes. "Why was he all in my face? I don't need his help."

"He means no harm. He's a nice guy. Not everyone is Ashton, J," Jo says.

"Not my type. I'm good."

"Whatever, both of you. Let's go," Mel says pushing them all out of the door.

I shake my head and go to get dressed. I make note to sit down with JC and have a talk. It sounds like she's becoming jaded from her breakup. She doesn't have to date Hershel, but it seems like she's closing herself off and I worry about that with her.

She had the hardest time adjusting when they lost their mom. She's a beautiful young woman. I tried to tell her Ashton wasn't for her. The boy was all about himself.

***

"Oh, look at this place. I want to go in this one," JC sings as we walk through town.

After dropping off Jack's truck, me and the girls came into town to do a little shopping. They have all chosen a room at the house and staked their claim.

"You would want to go into the first bakery we see," Mel says and rolls her eyes as she holds the door open for us all.

I'm the last to walk in as I have been here before. Shelby's is a cute little bakery that used to be a diner. The owner Alice is a sweet older woman.

"Oh, Coral. Welcome back, dear," Alice sings and clasps her hands together the moment she sees me.

"Hello, Alice. I have my daughters with me this time. This is Jo, JC, and Mel."

"Let me guess, Josephine, Melanie or Melissa and … let me think," Alice says while tapping her chin.

Jo laughs. "You got Melanie's name right. I'm Jodie but I can't remember the last time someone called me that."

"I'm actually Jodie too. Our moms both loved the name. My middle name is Cadence, so everyone started calling me JC when Jodie two was born," JC says good naturedly.

A confused look comes to Alice's face and I can't help but snicker. I know right away she's confused as I called the girls my daughters. We get that a lot.

"Jo is my biological daughter. Mel and JC are my nieces. Although I've had them since my sister passed when they were little. They are more like my daughters than my nieces, so I call them such," I explain.

"Oh, I'm sorry. You didn't have to explain. I didn't mean to show my confusion on my face."

"You're good. People ask all the time but how did you know those were all nick names?" Mel says.

"I'm Al to most. A habit I've been trying to break folks out of for years," Alice says with a warm smile. "I have some warm brownies fresh out the oven. What can I get for you ladies?"

"This place is so cute," JC says as she looks around.

"Thank you. I've loved it since the day I bought it. However, it's becoming a lot for me and the traffic hasn't been what it used to be."

"Oh really? What's changed in the area?"

"There used to be a day care a few blocks down. Kelly-Sue got engaged to some young fella she met on that there internet and she shut the place down and moved away. The town is now out of a day care and I'm out of the morning and afternoon rush. We've been losing a few businesses around here.

"I'm holding on as long as I can, but it's not looking too good for me. I'm going to either have to sell or close the doors and rent the place to someone else."

I watch as JC's eyes light up. I already know she has an idea brewing. Giving her a nod, I hold my thoughts and words to myself.

"I'll take a dozen of the chocolate chip cookies and another dozen of the oatmeal and raisin," Jo says.

"Is that fudge?" Mel asks.

"Yes, dear, it is. It's a town favorite."

"I'll take a half pound of the fudge. Make that a pound," Mel says.

"Coming right up. Coral, I heard you were looking at the old Riverwood place. How did you like it?"

"That's the little yellow house, right?"

"Not sure if I'd call it little, but yes. That's the one."

"It was nice but I'm purchasing Willowbrook."

"Oh my, if you're purchasing that place, I guess Riverwood is small in comprehension. I never thought I'd see the day Jack Harrington would let that place go. It's such a beautiful house."

"That it is."

"Oh, boy. Here comes trouble. I'll get you guys out of here as fast as I can," Alice whispers, causing us all to turn to the door as the bell rings over it.

In walks a woman with dark hair and blue eyes. She's curvy and a bit taller than I am. I'm about five-six. She has to have four inches on me.

"Hello, Alice. I've missed this place while in Paris. I just got back and had to come in for some of your coffee and fudge bars," the woman says.

"I'll be right with you, Betty-Lou. Let me get these girls squared away. Anything else, ladies?"

"Can I get a dozen of those muffins?"

"Sure, you can."

The bell over the door rings again and I turn to see who comes in. A smile breaks across my face as Jack and Chance saunter in. I'm surprised when Jack walks straight over to me and pulls me into his arms, then plants a kiss on my lips.

"Hey you, what are you doing here?'

"Had a craving for some of those orange and cranberry muffins. I thought I'd come get some for the B&B and get a few to bring over to Willowbrook for you ladies," he croons before kissing me once again.

"Hello, Jack," Betty-Lou says.

Jack turns to look in her direction as if just noticing her in the shop. He moves to my side and places an arm around me. I don't miss how Betty-Lou follows the motion with her eyes.

"Oh, where are my manners. I'm Betty-Lou Fantan. I don't believe we have met. You are …"

"Coral Marks. It's nice to meet you."

"Oh, the new librarian I've been hearing about. You must take my card. I'm sure you're looking to rent an affordable place to stay," she says and pulls her card.

"Actually, she's just purchased Willowbrook. Cash is handling the sale," Jack says.

"And how do you two know each other? Jack, did you recommend your friend here to Flo?"

"No. It was fate. Coral walked right into the B&B, and we hit it off."

"But I thought you weren't ready to date. You also said you would never sell Willowbrook. I mean, what all has suddenly changed?"

"She's not you and you're not her," Mel says with her hands on her hips.

"I know that's right," JC adds.

"Well, now. I never said I would never sell Willowbrook. What I told you was that I wasn't going to sell to those darn developers you came to me on behalf of. As far as my relationship with Coral that ain't none of anyone's business but hers and mine," Jack says firmly.

"See now, I knew I liked him," Mel sings.

"Jack … I … I never. I thought—"

"Ma'am please. Just stop embarrassing yourself. My mom has been more than polite," JC says.

"You're her daughter?" Betty-Lou scoffs.

"They all are," Alice says proudly.

"Figures."

"Oh, no you didn't. Listen, Miss. I don't like you already. You see my mom or any of us in this town, you cross the street. Don't make me dress you down and tell you about yourself.

"I already have words for how you assumed my mom needed to rent "affordable" and not buy," Jo says using air quotes. "Step aside and pick up your dignity. He was never interested."

Jack tugs me in closer and kisses the top of my head. Betty-Lou's face turns bright red. I try my best not to laugh, but Alice's muffled snickers almost make me lose it.

"You have a good day, Betty-Lou," Jack says, dismissing her.

I guess, that's that. Alice hands over our orders and gives Jack two boxes of muffins while she's at it. Me and my girls go to pay, but Jack covers it all and winks at the girls.

CHAPTER FOURTEEN

Fair of Fairytales

Coral

"Where would you like these?" Mayor Cash asks as he and a few of the other guys steps into the townhall building where we're still setting up for the festival festivities.

We've been working on this event for months. Everyone is excited and we're hopeful as JC's non-for-profit agreed to pick up some of the fundraising if this event goes over well. I can't even begin to express how proud of the girls I am.

I couldn't have done this on my own. Each of them has stepped in and played a part in pulling this all together. I know Cash is grateful for all the help he's gotten over the last four months.

Mel has been a great help to him not only with the fundraising, but she's been helping him out at the mayor's office as well. It's like we've all become a part of Spring Valley. Even though the girls go back and forth to handle their real lives and jobs.

"You can take that right over there with the rest of the boxes." I point.

He nods for the guys to follow him, and they place the boxes where I tell them to. Jo and a few volunteers get right on sorting things out. She and JC run a tight ship just as I like it. I can always count on them.

"I really can't thank you and the girls enough," Mayor Cash says. "When y'all offered to help, I didn't think y'all would show up like this."

"I just hope it will make a difference," I say.

"I'm hearing folks have been talking about this festival for weeks now as far as four towns over to the east and west of us. I'm more concerned about fire safety zones and crowd control."

"Fingers crossed we'll have that kind of turn out. I'd rather have to turn folks away or rotate than have empty booths and events." I sigh and place my hands on my hips.

"I have faith in you ladies. What Mel has done with my office is nothing short of a miracle. Is she around?"

"She and JC went to get into their costumes. Speaking of which." I turn to place my eyes on Jo. "Jo, honey. You better get going soon."

"Ugh, I know, Mom. Two of the venders arrived late and that's throwing everything off. Even though we built in two hours as a cushion.

"I just need to make sure these boxes get over to booth 350 and Booth 280 asked for an extension cord. I'll get ready as soon as I make sure they get what they need. Someone else will have to take over my checklist," she replies.

"I can take those boxes and the extension cords," Mayor Cash says.

"I'll handle the checklist," Chance adds.

"Jo, let them help. You go on and get ready."

"Okay, Mom. Thanks, Guys."

"You guys sure did go all out. I wasn't expecting the costumes. You look great, by the way. Has Pop seen you yet?" Chance says.

"No, I haven't seen him since he dropped us off this morning. The costumes were a nice idea to convey how Spring Valley is a magical place. We want everyone from out of town to leave with a lasting impression. You'll see," I say with a smile.

"Coral?"

I turn to find Jack staring at me with his mouth hanging open. I fully face him with a smile on my lips. He pulls a hand down his face and swallows hard as he moves his gaze over me.

I smooth a hand down my front. The corset the girls put me in is tight, but tasteful with its rich colors. It's blue, purple, teal, and coral.

Beautiful feathered matching wings spout from my back. I have on a chained crown over my hair that the girls brought in someone to straighten and add extensions to this morning bring my just below the shoulder length hair to locks down pass my butt.

I look all the part of a majestic fairy queen. Mel and I came up with the idea while reading a book with Emma. It's perfect. There are so many things that are magical about living in Spring Valley.

Spring Valley's Festival of Fairies and Magic will be a full experience. Food from the local restaurants, rides, game booths, and a live concert that will run throughout the day. JC and Mel were able to call in a few favors to get us some great names to perform and rotate throughout the day while drawing a great crowd.

The girls and I will greet the opening crowd and then spread out with the actors who volunteered. However, from the look on Jack's face, I can't help but wonder if I look as cool as everyone has said since I finished with the makeover.

"Hey, Jack."

"Darlin', can we have a talk?"

"I . . . I should get to the front of the festival."

"Yeah, I hear you, but this will only take a sec."

I purse my lips as I look at the time. I still have some time before I need to be up front. I'll have to ride in one of the carts to get there, but I should be fine.

Jack

I damn near swallowed my tongue when I walked in here and placed eyes on Coral. She looks fantastic. They've blended white extensions into her dark hair, and her makeup is flawless.

The little gems on her face only enhance her beauty. The costume is tasteful but sexy as sin. It all takes about twenty years off her age.

"What did you want to talk about?" Coral asks as we enter the small office.

I crowd her space and cup the side of her face. She looks up at me with her big bright eyes, and I can't hold myself back. I crush her lips with mine in a searing kiss.

She moans into my mouth and clings to the front of my shirt. I groan and wrap my arms around her to pull her closer. I deepen the kiss as I get carried away.

"Jack," she says breathlessly as she breaks the kiss.

I clear my throat and take a step back. Placing a hand to my lips, I try to regain my sense. I feel the blush that comes to my cheeks as we both breathe heavily.

"I'm sorry. I got carried away. I just wanted to tell you how amazing you look.

"Not sure I'm going to like you walking around like that all day, but I'll be happy to take you home and just knowing you're mine is going to give this old man an ego boost for the ages."

She laughs and cups the side of my face as she looks up into my eyes. The smile she gives me lights up her face and the room. My heart swells at the sight.

These last four months have brought me more joy than I can express. I look forward to our time together. The more time I spend with her the more time I want to have to dedicate to us.

Our banter keeps me on my toes. She cooks a delicious meal, and our nights give me new life. Just thinking about tonight has my blood pumping.

"I only have eyes for you, Jack. Now can I get to my station?"

"Of course, darlin'. I'm on transport. I'll get you there myself."

"Do you have a headset? I want to make sure I can get in touch with you for our balloon ride. You are going up with me, aren't you?"

I've been up in a hot air balloon once. I promised myself I'd never do it again, but that smile on her face is going to prove me a liar today.

"I sure am. I'll save a spot on my dance card tonight for some line dancing with you too."

"I can't wait. I'll let you know when my breaks are. Maybe we can catch a ride or two and it would be nice if my beau could win me a stuffed animal from one of the games."

"Your man plans to take care of you, sweetheart. Don't you worry about a thing."

I tug her into me for one more kiss. It's quick so we don't get carried away and I can get her to her station to open the festival. I groan as she goes to walk out ahead of me.

Lord, this is going to be a long day.

CHAPTER FIFTEEN

Companionship

Coral

I haven't smiled and laughed this hard in years. The festival is a great success. People have come out from all over. The local businesses have given a great representation of what this town has to offer.

I haven't seen a face that hasn't worn a smile. Not even Old Man Jerry, who always has a frown. I didn't expect to have a chance to truly enjoy the event myself, but Mayor Cash has made sure all of us have gotten to experience the festival for ourselves.

"That was amazing," I say to Jack as we exit the hot air balloon.

"It was. It went a little faster than I thought it would. You want to check in with the girls?"

"I just received a text. I have another hour before I need to hit my next station. You want to grab a bite or take in some of the music?"

"Sounds good. Ben has chili going over in the tent with the dancing and band. His recipe is award winning. You'll love it."

"I'm in. I love a good chili," I say and loop my arm through his.

"Y'all did great. This turn out is something else and everyone seems to be enjoying themselves. This brings back so many memories."

"Good ones, I hope."

"Nothing but. Mrs. Maggie used to run events like this before she passed away. That's when Lisa took over. I can't believe the town didn't step up to keep it all going sooner."

"I sure hope it helps. We have more ideas, but this is the kind of start we were hoping for."

"I don't think you have a thing to worry about. You captured the spirit of Spring Valley. The car show, the food, the dancing and entertainment," he says with a smile as he looks down at me.

"It's hard not to fall in love with this place. I'm happy to help. Besides, Cash is such a sweetheart. From what Mel says, he does so much for the town without saying a word.

"Really going above and beyond being the mayor. I want this to be a success for him if nothing else. He deserves it."

"That he does. You sit right here. I'll go get us some of that chili."

"Thank you, Jack."

He leans in and pecks my lips. "You don't have to thank me for a thing, darlin'. I'm having the time of my life. I should be thanking you."

"You can thank me later if you really feel you need to," I purr.

"You don't have to ask me twice."

He pecks my lips again and takes off to get our food. My belly growls letting me know that muffin and orange juice from this morning are long gone and I need some fuel sooner rather than later. I sit at the picnic table and begin to people watch.

"This turn out has been lovely, but I'm still confused on why grown men and women are walking around like it's Halloween and they're toddlers or adolescents."

I turn toward the snarky remark and the person it has come from. I'm not surprised to find Betty-Lou. She's been a bitch since the day I met her. Not a thing has changed.

Every time Jack and I see her in town, she gives me the evil eye. I've been ignoring her for the most part. She's a bitter woman. That's her problem, not mine.

I look her over in her pink outfit that her midsection is in a fight against. It's so ill-fitting as if she purchased the outfit in the dark and bought it two sizes too small. I would never body shame a woman, but the way she's looking me up and down like I'm the most disgusting thing ever to her, I can't help but take notice of her poor choice of clothing today.

Betty-Lou has an attractive face, but her attitude makes her very ugly. I already have Jack. I'm not about to go back and forth with this woman.

Instead, I turn away as if she's not even there. I smile when I hear her huff behind me. Some people don't deserve a response and Betty-Lou is one of those people.

"All these big name performers, I hope this event isn't going to set the town back," she continues, not catching a hint.

"Hey, Miss Coral. Here's your chili. Pop's getting you guys a couple of beverages. You need anything else?" Chance asks as he comes and places two bowls of chili down on the table, along with utensils.

"No, this is fine. Please, I told you before it's just Coral. Thank you, Chance."

"No ma'am. That's Miss Coral. Pop still has Ma's wooden spoon and he's not shy to use it.

"Just last year he got after Hersh when he left the t tractor out right before a big storm when Pop told him a hundred times to get after it. I never laughed so hard in my life. That is until Pop looked at me like I was next for laughing. Miss Coral it is," Chance chuckles.

"Well, thank you for the chili. I won't force you to have your daddy after you."

"No problem. Thank you, ma'am. You mind if I sit?"

"No, go right ahead."

"Hello, Miss Fantan. How are you enjoying the festival?"

"I was just telling Miss Coral here that the turnout is great, but I can't help wondering if too much money was spent. I also don't get the adults walking around in costumes. Seems childish if you ask me," she says smugly.

"Actually, the costumes make a lot of sense. Not only do the ladies look great in them, the kids have been in awe of every fairy they've encountered and have already begun to beg their parents to return.

"Spring Valley is a place of wonder and joy for the most part. The ladies nailed that with every detail of the festival today. The visual of all the fairies will stick with many and the entertainment was a nice touch.

"Not that it's any of your business but I heard the town hasn't had to come out of its pockets for any of this. Folks donated time, money, and resources. It's all spectacular," Chance says proudly.

"Oh, well. I was just concerned about the town. I guess it is a good thing. I have given out all my business cards and had a few inquiries about homes in the area," she stammers.

I stifle a laugh as I roll my eyes, still sitting with my back to Betty-Lou. Chance winks at me. I can't help the wide smile that comes to my face as Jack place drinks down on the table, then takes a seat beside me.

"Good evening, Jack. It's good to see you," Betty-Lou says.

"Good evening, Betty-Lou. I was just in line with a nice young couple. They're interested in moving here, you should go catch them before it's too late. I saw Jackson buzzing about earlier."

"That weasel. Why can't he stay on his own side of town," she grumbles and storms off.

"Ugh, thank you. You're a lifesaver. That woman tries to take me out of character every time I encounter her," I groan.

"She better watch it. Jo and Mel are chomping at the bit to tear her a new one," Jack chuckles.

"That's for sure. I've never seen this side of her. It's nasty and unbecoming. She used to seem so nice," Chance says.

Jack snorts while he tucks into this chili. I take my first spoonful and moan. It's so flavorful.

"Good, isn't it?" Jack says.

"It's delicious," I say as I cover my mouth.

"Lisa tried to get the recipe from Ben for years. He never budged."

Jack's eyes light up as he seems to fall into the memory. I place a hand on his back and give a rub. He turns to look me in the eyes and smiles.

"This makes me remember when we were little," Hershel says as he comes over and takes a seat.

"I know, right," Chance says as he bobs his head to the music.

"Oh my God, is that chili?" Jo groans as she sits down next to Chance.

"Yeah, you want some. I'll get you a bowl and a beer."

"My feet are killing me. You would be such a lifesaver. Cash told us to take the rest of the night to join the festivities."

"No worries, I've got you."

I smile as Chance winks at Jo and jumps up to get her a bowl of chili. Hershel stands and follows him. I take note that the tent is starting to fill, and the music has gotten a little louder.

"You did a good thing here, Coral. A real good thing."

"You can say that again," Mayor Cash croons as he appears with JC and Mel. "We just counted the donations. We tripled the goal. I'll be able to buy out Jenkins and have something in reserve for the next property."

"I'd say we pulled another one off, Mom. My office sent me a text. They're going to take on the next project," JC sings.

"That's wonderful," I say happily.

"How about a dance to celebrate?" Jack says and stands.

Chance and Hershel return with a tray of chili and beers for everyone. I smile as my girls sit with Jack's boys and begin to chat excitedly. This move has been great for my family.

My girls know they always have a place to come to and get away from the stress of the world. A happy place that's what Spring Valley has become.

I stand and place my hand in Jack's. He leads me to the dance floor and tugs me into his arms. I melt into his embrace as we sway to the music.

"I almost forgot what this all feels like," Jack murmurs.

"What's that?"

"Happiness."

"Yeah, I know what you mean."

"You showed up right when I needed you. I hate to admit it, but I wasn't there for my boys like I needed to be. I see that now. I guess that's why they were pushing me to date."

"Let me guess. Betty-Lou was on their list of potentials," I snicker.

"I don't know about their list, but the woman sure did have a list of her own."

I laugh from deep in my belly. "That she does. I don't think she's let it go."

"She better. You're stuck with me, darlin'. Home is where the heart is, and you've made this home again for us all."

I place my head against his chest and sigh. There isn't anywhere else I'd rather be. Spring Valley has brought me so much peace.

This has become something I didn't know I needed.

Jack

"Wow, these things are heavier than I thought. How did you walk around with them on your back all day?" I ask as I grab Coral's wings from the backseat of my truck.

"Ugh, I do think I'll have bruises in the morning. I'll be sore if nothing else."

"Then let me get you inside and into a bath. I'll massage your shoulders for you."

"That sounds wonderful."

We make our way into the house and head straight for her bedroom. When we spend the night together, we usually stay here at Willowbrook. I won't say anything, but I don't think I'm ready for us to be intimate at the B&B.

I've come a long way, but I don't know if I've come that far. I count my blessings that Coral seems to get that and has never suggested we spend time at the B&B during our evenings.

"You can place those in the closet. I'll get the bath started," Coral says as she heads into the en suite.

I step into the closet and go to set the wings down. However, as I go to exit the closet something catches my eye. I had forgotten about the old blankets Lisa made and had me bring over here to store.

My feet are carrying me over to them before I can tell my brain what to do next. I pull one from the shelf and bring it to my nose. Tears burst from my eyes as Lisa's scent hits my nose. Inhaling deeply, I slide down to the floor sobbing.

I try to stifle my sobs, but I can't. I begin to hyperventilate. My heart aches so bad, I feel lost.

"Jack, honey? Are you okay? What's going on?"

I shake my head not having the words to speak. Coral comes to sit on the floor with me and wraps her arms around me. As she coos and rocks me from side to side, I try to pull it together.

"It's going to be all right. Shh, relax. Breathe."

Suddenly, this all feels so wrong. "I'm sorry. I need to go. I'm sorry."

Still clenching the blanket, I pull away and climb to my feet. Swallowing hard, I shake my head and rush from the house like a fire is on my ass. I need space and a chance to breathe.

CHAPTER SIXTEEN

Things Change

Jack

"What's going on, old friend? A week ago, I would have said I haven't seen you so happy in years. Now you look like someone kicked your puppy," Terry says as we sit on the porch of the B&B.

"Nothing happened. I'm fine."

"Now you don't believe that any more than I do. What's going on?"

"Nothing. I have a lot to be grateful for. The girls have brought new life to Spring Valley. The town has never been busier and that's bringing plenty of business in on all fronts."

"But …"

"But what?"

"That little librarian is something else. The whole town loves her. I didn't expect the changes to reach out to my edge of town but that book bin idea of hers was genius.

"I rent boats by the hour. Them folks are picking up books and sitting out on the water getting lost in the pages. Almost fifty percent of the rentals have started to book additional hours or have ended up paying late fees. Happily, might I add.

"Doesn't matter the gender either. The thriller bin works as good as the romance one. Didn't know folks still love to get lost in pages," Terry chuckles.

"She's good at what she does, and she loves it. She and those girls have this light about them that I think we all needed. They're just full of ideas."

"I can see that, but that leads me back to my main question. You two were going strong and you were so happy. What happened?"

"I had somethings I needed to figure out. I want to be fair to Coral. I thought I was ready, but … I don't know anymore."

Terry sighs. "I know how hard it is to move on. I cried like a baby the first time I was intimate with someone after losing Marly. Took a long time to get there, but when I did the guilt and confusion took me over."

"That's just it. I didn't feel guilt when we started having relations. I've been fine for months.

"The night of the festival, I found some of Lisa's blankets in the closet. One whiff and I broke. What if this isn't what Lisa wanted? What if I made all that up in my head because I wanted it?"

"Jack, we've been friends for a really long time. I knew your wife as well as I know you. Lisa would have wanted this for you. For you to be happy.

"I mean, listen to you talk about her girls like a proud father. That's what I meant, a week ago, you were happy about more than what's going on in Spring Valley.

"You're in love again, and that's okay. This isn't some fling. You're open to letting someone in. It's really good to see, buddy. Allow yourself this. Make peace with them feelings and get back to living again.

"You were happier, and the boys seemed like they had less weight on their shoulders. If nothing else, Lisa would want you to do this for them."

I pause for a moment. It's been four months since Coral moved into Willowbrook and settled into her new job. The girls come and go as their jobs allow them, but they're here more than not as they've been working tirelessly with Cash to turn things around.

I've even noticed that Cash hasn't been running himself into the ground as much. My boys do seem happier as well, but can I say I'm in love? I don't know.

Last week put me in my feelings. I sobbed myself to sleep holding that blanket. I haven't really spent a lot of time with Coral since.

She still means a whole lot to me. Our talks and walks used to be the highlight of my day. Our nights were only the icing on the cake.

I had no idea I could be so insatiable, but Coral doesn't complain. Our sex life is so passionate and enthralling. She makes me feel alive again.

However, I don't know how to move forward just yet. The last thing I want is to hurt her. Terry is right. I do need to sort my feelings and deal with the situation.

"I don't know if I can say I'm in love. Yes, I care for her deeply," I murmur.

"Oh, you're in love all right. You might not have realized it yet, but I see the way you look at her. There's nothing wrong with it either.

"I'm only saying that I'm happy for you and it looks good on you. When you allow yourself to have it, I think Lisa would be proud of you for trying."

"There was a time when I did too."

"I know it's hard but try to get back there. I know your boys are happy for you. To be honest, I've been coming around more because this place is filled with joy these days. Makes me feel good to be around," he says with a big smile.

"Glad to have you around more. You sticking around for dinner this time?"

"Nope, if I'm hearing right, you need to have a sit down with Coral. I'm not about to start playing the third wheel. Besides, I have a hot date of my own. I should be heading out to go get ready."

I smile as I watch my old friend stand and stretch. I chuckle to myself as his bones snap, crackle, and pop. I better get up from here soon myself.

"Who's your hot date with?"

"Jennifer Morrison. She got me with that peach cobbler," he says and pats his stomach.

I chuckle and shake my head. Jennifer does make a fine cobbler. She makes it for most of the town events. Has won a ribbon or two too.

I tug Terry into a hug. We pat each other on the back and pull apart. As he walks off to his truck, I can't help but think over our conversation.

Could I be in love again and I just haven't allowed myself to acknowledge it? I continue to muse as I head into the B&B in search of something to do before Coral gets off from work. I think we should have dinner and a chat.

"Pop, you got a minute?"

I turn to find Chance staring at me with a perplexed look on his face. This young fella has caused me to worry about him more and more lately. His brother isn't doing too much better.

"Sure, son. Come on in my office. We can talk in there."

We walk into my office. I round my desk to have a seat as Chance takes the seat across from me. I take note of his new haircut and the fact that his clothes look brand-new.

"What's going on, son?"

He blows out a long breath as he wipes his hands up and down his thighs, revealing his nerves. "It's Jo. I can't help thinking about something Miss Coral once said." He pauses to run his hand through the front of his hair.

"I love the friendship I have with Jo. She's smart and she makes me laugh but I think she's placed me permanently in the friendzone. What I'm trying to say is, I want more.

"I want to date her, but her mom says I should be direct with her or she's not going to see how I feel. I was okay with being in the friendzone when I thought Hershel was interested as well.

"Now, I want to pursue her, but I want to be respectful. How can I be direct without crossing her boundaries?"

"Son, you're thinking too hard. Just like you're sitting here talking to me. You need to sit her down and do the same thing."

"Yeah, but things have been so hectic with her going back and forth for work and helping with all the fundraising and stuff. It feels like there's never a right time."

I snort. "How about when you two are snuggled on the couch at Willowbrook watching movies and eating popcorn. Seems like that happens at least once every other week."

He groans. "You sure this is all right with you and Mrs. Coral? Me dating her daughter."

"All I hear are excuses, Chance. What's the real problem?"

He chews on his jaw a bit as he stares into his palm and rubs his thumb across his skin. After a few moments of silence, he lifts his blue gaze to mine, reminding me of when he was a little boy.

However, I see the man he's becoming shine through. As the youngest of my two, he's always been ambitious and outgoing. I love that about him as much as he can get on my nerves.

"I've always been that guy. In high school all it took was a wink and I got the girl. Jo is different. She either really doesn't see how crazy I am about her, or she's not interested at all.

"I've watched you and Mama up until the very end and now I see you in love again. I want that. I think Jo is the one for me to have that with. I'm just terrified of blowing it, if I'm honest."

I stare at my son for a moment. His words shocking me. That's two people in one day who have mentioned that I'm in love.

"Never mind, Pop. You taught us not to let life pass us by. I need to do what you always say."

"What do I say?"

"Follow your heart. Don't let your mind rob you of what your heart wants and needs. Thanks, Pop. I've got this."

I nod as those words sink in. They were words my daddy used to tell me. I grunt to myself and pull a hand down my face.

"I'll be damn. I think I need a nap," I murmur into the now empty room.

Coral

"What's going on, Mom?" Mel asks as she comes to sit with me in the living room at the house.

"Nothing, honey. Just a lot on my mind."

"Is this about Jack? I noticed you two have cooled way down. What's that about?"

"I wish I knew. One-minute things were fine, then he had a breakdown in my closet, and he's been avoiding me since."

"You know I was worried about you dating a widower. It's not like your divorce. You and Uncle Ralph made a choice to part ways.

"Mr. Jack lost his wife. I'm sure if he could have done something to keep her alive and with him, he would have. That has to hurt something awful.

"When Mommy died, I didn't think things would ever get right again. It was you. You turned things around for us. You made the bad days better.

"However, there were still days, moments, times when even with you there it felt like I wouldn't be able to breathe.

"Two things are always true at once. Mr. Jack is probably dealing with trying to understand that. He loved his wife and he's falling in love with you too.

"All I'm trying to say is … have patience. I don't think he's trying to hurt you intentionally. Jack is like all the rest of us, we're trying to find our way," Mel says.

"When did you get so wise? I'm so unbelievably proud of you, Mel. I see you, baby girl. You're such an amazing woman."

"Thanks, Mom. I've had the best example to glean from."

"How about we cut into that pie JC made and get into some ice cream?"

"Now you're talking," she sings.

CHAPTER SEVENTEEN

Setting You Free

Jack

"There you are. I've been waiting for you. We need to talk. It's time we have a heart to heart."

"Lisa?"

"Hello, Jack, my love. Have a seat."

I look around me at my surroundings. We're by the lake at the back of the property. This had been one of Lisa's favorite spots. She would sit out here by the water for hours.

I remember when the boys were younger. They would run around while Lisa would bask in the sun. She was always so beautiful and full of life.

I had thought I would get to watch her turn old and gray, needing my help to sit in the grass and get back up. Losing her put an end to my trips to this part of the property. I knit my brows as that comes to mind.

"Jack?"

I lift my gaze to hers. She looks perfect like no time has passed and she was never ill. I search her face with my eyes, afraid to reach out and touch her in fear she will disappear.

"I've missed you so much."

"I know. I know how much you're hurting, Jack. I see your pain. I never wanted this for you.

"You were so good to me … and our boys. I don't regret falling for you and spending my life with you. I wouldn't change a second, but my time has come to an end, Jack.

"My time, not yours. You still have so much life to live. Our boys are watching you for their answers to what's next."

"I'm doing my best, darlin'. I'm trying to breathe. It's just so hard."

"I know. If the shoe was on the other foot, I don't know if I ever would find another man who would make me feel like you did. I get it.

"However, the creator had other plans for you. You have found your second chance. Your other half.

"That flame that's burning is one for the ages. You and Coral were meant to be. That's why I'm setting you free, Jack.

"I will always be in your heart, but your heart beats for another whether you know it yet or not. I meant what I said, my love. I need you to live your life and be happy.

"Great things are in Spring Valley's future. I'm gone but the magic of our town is still well and alive."

"I don't know if she'll have me after what I've done. I messed everything up," I choke out.

"Did you? You know something, Jack. True love has a way of being patient and kind. And you, my love, are a fierce and passionate lover. You have not lost this battle but it's time you begin to fight it."

"I hope you're right," I murmur.

"Ah, you're still as stubborn as ever. This isn't just a dream, Jack. You will know this is my farewell.

"That box I gave you and told you not to open until you were ready … you're ready. It's time to open your future. It's my final parting gift. I love you, Jack."

"I love you too, darlin'. You rest well. I've got our boys."

"I know you do. Give them a hug for me."

She leans into me and brushes my cheek with her lips. I close my eyes and bask in the feeling as my heart fills with love.

"Be happy, Jack. Breathe and be happy, my love. Goodbye."

I pop up from my sleep and palm my forehead. That dream felt so real. I had only laid down for a quick nap before Coral gets home from work, and I can talk to her.

As the fog clears, I try to hold onto everything Lisa said. A glance at the clock pulls a groan from my lips. Those boys let me sleep too long. I should've woken hours ago.

Coral is sure to have gotten home, had supper, and gone to bed by now. I knit my brows as I remember the box Lisa talked about in the dream. Climbing from the bed, I head over to the chest I tucked the box away in.

I get down on my knees and rummage through the bottom drawer. When I get my hands on the box, I stumble to my feet and amble back over to the bed and flop down on it. Until that dream, I had forgotten all about this box.

I run a hand over the top. Once Lisa died, I wasn't ready to take this lid off. I was drowning so deep in my grief, I never thought the time would come when I would be able to.

My hands tremble as I remove the lid. Placing it aside, I look into the box and pull out the letter resting on the top. It's on the pretty paper I purchased about a month before Lisa passed away.

Dear Jack,

I know you will struggle once I'm gone. It's my hope that if you're reading this, you are ready. It's time, Jack. It's okay. Whoever she is, she must be special. What I know for a fact is that you deserve happiness.

You have so much love to give and you deserve to be loved. In this box you will find a gift I thought I would share with your new love. It's my peace offering.

I don't hate her, and I could never hate you. All I want for you is love and happiness.

You remember that one time, Terry and Marly made sure we danced the night away? Those were good times.

I want you to make more memories with this lovely woman who has captured your heart.

I know you have found her and you're in love because you never would have been ready for this step if you hadn't. Things are going to be as they should be. Don't hold back, don't feel any guilt, and don't leave any regrets.

Live well, Jack, but most of all, live. I love you.

Love always,
Lisa

I smooth a hand over the page before placing it aside and digging out the other items in the box. My heart fills with love and warmth. I can't help but release a deep belly laugh as I go through everything in the box.

"You were the best, Lisa. I get your message loud and clear, darlin'. I hear you loud and clear."

I continue to laugh as I shake my head. It might be too late tonight, but I'm going to make this right.

CHAPTER EIGHTEEN

Caution Given

Coral

I wake up thirsty and ready for breakfast. Climbing out of bed, I then head for a shower. I have the day off and want to get some reading done. I also want to look over our plans for the next fundraising event.

Once I'm fully dressed, I look at my phone and think about calling Jack. Quickly, I shake the thought off and decide to give him space to sort his feelings out. My stomach growls letting me know nothing else is that important at the moment.

"I can't believe he would do this. You warned me but I thought I had it all under control. I'm the damn mayor, of course I didn't buy all that land in my name, but if he keeps digging, he's going to find my fingerprints all over those deeds," a male growls as I make my way toward the kitchen.

"Cash, you have to calm down. You did right coming to me. We can fix this. I know what you said, but I looked into the best courses of action after I learned how much of the land you took ownership of yourself," Mel says as I turn the corner.

"Hey, is everything all right?"

"No," Mayor Cash bites out. "This shit has come back to bite me. Someone tipped my daddy off to the Jenkins purchase. He came over to the house huffing and puffing and threatening."

"Oh my God, I had no idea Courtland could be such a jerk. Why is he so hell-bent on helping those developers take over this town?"

"I have no damn idea. I would think he would want to save it as much as I do," he huffs.

"I'm not much on property law or mayoral conflicts of interest, but my ex-husband is a property attorney. How about a deed transfer or something? Isn't that what it's called?"

"She's right, that's what I was going to suggest. If you have someone you trust, someone this town means as much to that you can transfer some of the properties to. It doesn't have to be everything, you just shouldn't be holding as much as you have …"

Cash pulls a hand down his face. "Uncle Jack and my cousins are the only ones I can trust. I mean, other than you ladies."

"That will work. Push comes to shove, I'll take a few properties off your hands. We can draw up an agreement or something if you like."

"Not if my daddy gets to the clerk before we can handle all the paperwork."

"Thank God, it's the weekend and a three day one at that. That gives us three days."

"I'll call Ralph. I'm sure he'll come in and give us some help. All we'll need is a notary," I reply.

"Ashley is a high school friend she lives a town over, but I can give her a call and see if she's available."

"Good, we can file all the paperwork first thing Tuesday morning before your father has a chance to blow the whistle."

Cash nods. "Give me a sec to make the call."

"I'll call Ralph." I turn to head back to my bedroom for my phone.

The breakfast I had been going for is forgotten. It's early on a Saturday morning but I'm hoping Ralph will do me this favor. I feel terrible as it's a long drive, but I know how much this town means to Cash.

"Hello," Ralph says tiredly into the phone.

"I need a big favor."

"Coral? What's going on? Are the girls all right?"

"They're fine. I just have a young friend in a jam. Can you come out to Spring Valley and meet with a young man who's a friend of mine and Mel's? He has a few properties that need to change hands now."

"*Coral* … I'm retired but I still want to keep my license. What are you really asking for?"

"Cash Washington is the mayor. His father has been helping some developers try to buy the town out from under everyone. His father has gotten wind of properties that may or may not have come into Cash's possession," I explain.

"He has no ill intentions, but it still can be seen as a conflict of interest," Ralph sighs.

"Yes, and we only have until Tuesday morning to fix it."

"That's a six-hour drive, honey. I'm beat."

"Call a car, Ralph. I'll cover the cost, please."

"Don't worry about it. I'll see you in a bit, yeah?"

"Thank you," I breathe.

I hang up and head back to the kitchen to give Cash and Mel the news. My eyes widen when I find Emma at the island eating a bowl of cereal. I had no idea she was here with Cash.

"Ralph is on his way," I say brightly, even though inside my blood is boiling.

Courtland has a bad habit of throwing this drama at Cash when he's trying to raise his niece and be all she needs on top of trying to be the best mayor he can be. I could never treat my children this way. Especially not in front of my grandbabies.

“That’s great. Ashley will be here after she drops her kids off with their dad.”

“Okay, what’s next?

“I need to talk to Uncle Jack and the guys, but I was getting Emma ready for a birthday party in Sea View before my dad showed up.”

“I’ll take Emma to her party. You focus on getting everyone ready for when Ralph arrives.”

“Thank you so much, Miss Coral. I appreciate this,” Cash says.

“No thanks needed. Let me get dressed and I’ll get her to the party, no problem.”

“You don’t know how much this is helping me out. Do me a favor. Keep a watch on the weather.

“There’s been talk about that storm possibly turning this way. Sea View is known for flooding and roads washing out. Maybe I should take her, I’m concerned about your car,” Cash says with new concern written all over his face.

“It will be fine. Emma and I can use some fun. We’ll get out of you guys’ hair and have some fun at the party before we come back. I have your back. It’s all going to be fine.”

“I’ll make you some breakfast before you go,” Mel says. “Jo and JC are coming in this weekend. They should be here by the time you get back.”

“Maybe JC will decide to cook something for everyone when she gets here,” I muse.

“I’m sure she will.”

I nod and turn back for my room to get dressed. It’s been years since I’ve taken an eight-year-old to a birthday party. I remember always being one of the moms to pitch in. Having that thought, I get dressed in jeans and a T-shirt and toss on a pair of sneakers.

“Birthday party here we come,” I breathe to myself.

As long as Emma doesn’t have to sit around grown folks’ business, I’m happy to do my part. Going to a birthday party is the least I can do. I just hope this all works out.

Courtland

"We were this close to getting the Jenkins' property. I thought you said it would be a sure thing," I growl.

"It was a sure thing until Mayor Cash got in the way. I'm telling you, he's the one who's been buying everything up before we can get to it. If we don't turn things around soon, we're going to lose this opportunity. They're already looking elsewhere."

"Don't you think I already know that. Once I have a full investigation going, that will put an end to all of Cash's stunts."

"You were bluffing when you went to see him. Do you really think they will be able to find anything that proves he's the one buying everything?"

"I don't know," I bite out. "My son is smart. I doubt they will, but the implication might be just what we need.

"We're not the only ones who want to see this change happen. All we need are the right folks to get their panties in a bunch. I might have been bluffing, but your tip was spot on.

"There's something there. I saw it in his eyes. Hopefully, I rattled his cage enough for him to slip up," I grumble.

"I know why I'm doing this, but why are you so hell-bent on screwing over your own son?"

"I have my reasons. Spring Valley has never done a thing for me. I'm just collecting what I'm owed, and Cash's stubborn ass has gotten right in my way."

"This better not be a waste of my time, Courtland. That tip better not find its way back to me either. I'm warning you."

CHAPTER NINETEEN

Something's Wrong

Jack

"I want to thank you all for doing this for me," Cash says.

"You know we're here for you," Hershel says.

"Family looks after family," I reply.

Cash didn't have to ask twice for my help. I came right over to Willowbrook when he told me what's going on. However, I do have to say I was a bit disappointed when I arrived and Coral wasn't here.

Jo and JC arrived not too long after I did. I've been on pins and needles wondering where Coral is, but I haven't had the nerve to ask. When Chance and Hershel came over with Ralph, Coral's ex-husband, I was so blinded by jealousy, I missed when he was told where Coral is.

The man is not only handsome, I can tell he's well off and educated. His expensive looking watch and shoes are a far cry from my cowboy boots, T-shirts, and flannel shirts.

"That's the last one. I didn't know you were a realtor," Ralph says to Cash.

"For ten years before becoming the mayor here. I figured I'd make your job easier before you arrived so we could move right through things," Cash replies.

"Wow, that rain is picking up. Looks like I might need to wait it out before I try to head back," Ralph says as the rain begins to pound down harder outside.

"There are plenty of rooms at the B&B. It'll be on me. Thank you for coming to help my nephew," I say.

"If Coral or my girls call, I'm going to come running. Coral said Cash means something to her and Mel. Sure wasn't expecting to be out in that mess, but I made it happen.

"Glad I got in before it hit. I was hoping I'd get to see Coral before I make any decisions about heading back. Jodie, baby girl, have you spoken to your mother. This weather is staring to worry me."

"We've been trying to text her. I think the storm is interfering with service," Jo replies. "Cash, do you have the number for the party?"

"Wait a minute. Coral took Emma to that birthday party in Sea View? Boy, have you lost your mind. Why would you send them out there knowing that storm could turn?

"If they're getting this weather that way, she shouldn't be out on those roads. Sea View is known for flooding and the roads washing out."

"Awe, hell. Uncle Jack, I'm sorry. My head wasn't on straight, I wasn't thinking. They said there was only a twenty percent chance the storm would turn. I—"

Cash is cut off by his ringing phone. My chest tightens. Something is wrong. I know it before he answers the call.

"Erin, I have you on speaker. What's going on?"

"Thank God, I'm on my landline. I didn't think I would get through. It's that nice lady who brought Emma to the party.

"My stupid sister-in-law dropped Nancy's cake right as we were about to cut it. That Miss Coral left to pick up another one before the storm started. Last we spoke, she was on her way back with it.

"I haven't been able to reach her for the last hour. She hasn't made it back, Cash. I'm starting to get real worried.

"Emmy is still here with me, she's welcome to stay as long as she needs, but I thought I should give you a call about Miss Coral. I feel so bad," Erin says.

"That little car can't handle a storm like this," I growl and get to my feet.

"Thanks for the call, Erin. We're sending a search party. I'll make sure someone stays by the landline here at the house.

"Take down this number for me. We'll have walkie talkies and the CBs in the trucks. If you call someone can get through on the radios."

"Okay, I have a pen and paper. I'm ready when you are."

I'm heading for the door before he can get off the line. I need to find Coral and get her to safety. Cash should have known better.

"Pop, hold on. We should head out in teams," Chance calls after me.

"Whoever's coming with me better come on. I'm not wasting another minute."

I don't stop until I'm in my truck. To my surprise Ralph and Hershel jump in with me. I don't know that I can do this right now.

"Don't you think you should stay here with the girls?" I grumble.

"I've been volunteer emergency rescue for years. If anything, I can help."

I grunt and pull off in the direction of Sea View. I'm not going to leave behind anyone who can help Coral no matter how I feel. Now I see why he's as fit as I am while working behind a desk.

"Is this place far from here?" he asks.

"In this rain it could take us about an hour if the roads are clear."

"Take my phone. Keep trying her line," I say to Hershel.

"I still have her phone on Find My. Will that help?" Ralph says.

"Yeah, that will," Hersh replies and takes Ralph's phone.

"Looks like she's not moving. She's not that far from the shopping center near Erin's."

"Let Cash and the others know," I say as I push through the heavy rain in the direction of the shopping center in Sea View.

"I take it you're the gentleman Coral's been seeing," Ralph says after about ten minutes.

"Is that a problem?"

"No, and you shouldn't make it one. Coral is my best friend. We want different things in this stage of our lives but we're still friends and I care about her well-being.

"My Jo-jo has brought you up with nothing but kind words. I'm only asking to put a face to the situation. You seem concerned about her beyond that of the concern of a neighbor," he says.

"Coral and the girls have become like family. I'm always going to be concerned about them."

I leave it at that and focus on trying to see the road ahead of me. It's all I can do not to come apart before I get to her. The roads aren't looking good, and I still have this uneasy feeling.

Coral

"*Mm,*" I whimper as I lie trapped in my car.

This storm came out of nowhere. One minute I was heading back to the house with the cake, the next the road flooded right before my eyes.

A tree fell and the car heading toward me from the other direction swerved in front of me. I didn't have time to try to avoid the collision and the tree. The tree fell right across my car and trapped me inside.

I'm at an odd angle because I did dive out of the tree's way as it crashed down on my car. I can't reach my phone and I'm in so much pain. My head, wrist, shoulder, and ankle hurt so bad.

"Help," I struggle to call out.

I'm getting soaked from the rain coming in through the smashed window. I'm not sure if my vision is blurry from the crash or the rain pouring in.

I groan and shut my eyes. This is not how I thought my life would come to an end. I have so much I still want to impart in my girls, trips I want to take, things I want to say to Jack and Ralph.

I'm so angry I could scream. I'm a good person. Why is this happening?

I want to be a grandmother and be there to watch my grandbabies grow old. I want to help my girls with their veils and talk them through the hard times in life.

Jo still needs me so much and Mel and JC don't deserve to lose another mother. With this in mind, I fight against the darkness that's trying to take me under. Forcing my eyes back open, I try to call out again.

"Help, someone please help."

"Coral, darlin'. I'm here, baby girl. I'm going to get you out. Can you hear me? Talk to me, darlin'."

"Jack?" I croak out.

"I'm here, Coral. Help is on the way, but I'm going to get to you."

"Jack, we should wait for help. That's a big tree."

"Ralph?"

"Hey, honey. You all right in there?"

"I'm scared. I hit my head and my leg is trapped. I don't want our girls to lose me like this."

"Ain't nobody losing you today," Jack says sharply. "Hershel, you get those gloves out my truck and get on over here. Help me shift this tree out the way."

"Pop, you're not going to be any good to her if you give yourself a stroke or heart attack."

"I said help me. That's the woman I love in there. I'm not losing her. Help me now, boy."

"Jack, no. Listen to Hershel," I cry out.

"Baby, what good are two ranch hands if we can't move a little tree when we need to? We're going to get you out."

"Pop, you still have those chains in your truck?"

"Yeah, there's a chainsaw back there too."

"I can saw, you two can try to get the tree out of the way. I don't think we're getting in through the driver's side but if we work at the passenger's side, we might be able to get to her," Ralph says.

Tears run down my face as they make a plan to get me out. I don't have the mind to process that Jack said he loves me. As the chainsaw starts hope begins to bloom.

I don't know how much time passes but soon I'm looking into a pair of blue eyes as Jack and Ralph are able to pry the passenger door open.

Jack climbs in and gingerly brushes his hand over my face. He places his forehead to mine gently. I want to sob in relief as I know I at least won't die alone.

"Oh, baby. I'm sorry. I don't think we should move you. We're going to need some help getting that leg free and getting you out of here."

"I'm just happy I'm not alone."

"You will never be alone again. I'm so sorry for the way I've been acting. I just needed some time to sort my head out. I'm sorry.

"If I wasn't acting like an asshole, you wouldn't be here. I'd never forgive myself if I would have lost you too. I just found you and I know I can't live without you."

"You can't blame yourself. We'll talk when I get out of here, okay?"

"God, I don't deserve you. You hear that, baby? Help is here." He kisses my forehead. "I love you, Coral. As soon as you're better we're going to go on a date and I'm going to talk to you like an adult.

"It's time for me to heal before I lose you. I don't want to be a lonely fool for the rest of my life. Lisa wouldn't want that for me. I don't want that for us."

"I—"

"You don't have to say it back. I just needed you to know."

"Sir, we're going to need you to step back. We'll get her out from here."

Jack presses his lips to my forehead once again. When I shift my gaze, I lock eyes with Ralph who's giving me a tight smile. I try to return it. Ralph winks at me before he helps Jack back to his feet and they both move out of the way.

"Thank you, God," I breathe to myself.

I'm going to be here for my girls. I'm going to survive this.

CHAPTER TWENTY

Love Like This

Coral

Everyone has been so sweet and helpful while I've recovered from the accident and the storm. Flo has covered for me as I've been on leave.

I needed time for my dislocated shoulder to heal. My leg had only been swollen and bruised but thank God it wasn't broken. My wrist, however, was sprained and I had a concussion.

Jo took off from work for the first two weeks. From there JC took over since she's been in town for work. Ralph has called daily to check in.

I've had no shortage of visitors and helpers. Erin has even been by to thank me and let me know how bad she felt. I still feel bad for poor Nancy.

I watched her aunt drop that cake on purpose. Grown folks shouldn't drag children into their pettiness. It was clear Erin and her sister-in-law had some type of tension going on between them.

"Are you comfortable?" Jack asks.

We're in one of the private tasting rooms inside the brewery. The lighting and candlelight are setting a romantic vibe. Dinner was delicious.

We're finally having that date. It's been a little over a month, but Jack hasn't let a day go by without showing up at my door. He has brought by dinner and sat with me while I've rested and healed. However, we're never alone during his visits and we haven't been intimate in anyway.

"Yes, I'm fine. Please don't fuss over me," I reply.

"It's no fuss. I'm happy we're finally getting a moment alone."

"I know, it's like my house has become the hang out spot. I love having Emma over, but them grown folks act like they're all my babies," I snicker.

"It's true. My boys are in your home more than I've seen them in my own. It might have something to do with all the pretty women who stay there," Jack chuckles.

"Or JC's cooking and baking. I think Cash was over every night last week."

"That girl can cook. I think she missed her calling. She seems so happy when she's in the kitchen."

"We've been saying that for years. However, I don't think you wanted to have this date to talk about my niece and her ambitions," I say with a smile.

Jack blushes. "No, I didn't. I've been missing us. I want to explain what happened that night—"

"Jack, you don't have to explain. I think I understand."

"No, that ain't right. I handled things wrong. I want you to fully understand what was going on with me. Those blankets in your closet. I forgot they were there.

"Lisa knitted them while she was … going through everything. I broke down and got confused. I felt so much guilt.

"There I was getting ready to take a bath and make love to the woman I'm falling madly in love with, but in my hands, I held a labor of love from the woman I spent the better part of my life with.

"At the same time, I wasn't ready to admit that my feelings had gotten that far. I was in denial about where our relationship is heading. After having a talk with Terry and then Chance, I had some time to think about things and gain a fresh perspective.

"Then I had this dream. In the dream I was reminded of a box Lisa gave me before she passed. She told me to open it when I was ready. It was such a Lisa thing to do, but it helped me release the guilt I had been feeling," he explains.

"I love that for you."

"I did too. I got a good laugh and so much clarity. I had planned to come to you and apologize but then you weren't home when I arrived to sign those papers for Cash. Then the call came in that you were out in that storm.

"All I could think about was if I couldn't get to you, if none of us would find you in time and the chance I could lose you."

He pauses and swallows hard as he reaches across the table and takes my hands in his. He searches my eyes for a moment before he starts again.

"I would have been a fool lost all over again and you would have been gone before I could tell you how much I've fallen in love with you."

"Jack, I've fallen in love with you too. I had my own talk with Mel, and she made me see that you may have been dealing with those kinds of feelings. I know your situation is different from mine.

"This has to be hard for you. You were able to look my ex-husband in the eyes and have a conversation. I'd like to say you two have found a new friend in each other." I roll my eyes. "I'll never be able to say that about me and your wife."

"Actually, that's just it. You may never meet Lisa in the flesh, but to make sure I didn't get hung up on that fact, she'd been preparing me all along. I might not have wanted to listen, but she used subtle humor and talks to get me ready," he says.

"Oh really, how so? What do you mean?"

"There was this one time. Right around the time Lisa was too ill for intimacy. She joked about me finding a sister wife.

"Someone to take care of my needs until she was feeling up to it again. I'd been upset with her in the moment, but later we were able to laugh and joke about it. On another occasion, she mentioned wanting to gift her sister wife with something to tie them together as sisters.

"I'd forgotten all about that. Then I opened the box and found this inside with a little note for you. I laughed so hard my belly hurt.

"You don't have to take it if you don't want. I know it's more her way to make me feel okay with moving on," he says as he slides a box with a note on top toward me.

I open the note first as curiosity gets the best of me. A smile comes to my lips as I read the note. I wish I could have met this woman in person.

You must be amazing to be Jack's new love. I love you already for mending what I've broken. To be honest, I've always wanted a sister. Please accept this gift as a thank you and a little inside joke between the three of us. I know it will ease Jack's guilt every time he sees it, and it will make him smile. Hopefully you'll share in the humor. That is until the day you both decide to put it away and move on without me.

Love eternally your sister,
Lisa

Placing the note down, I then open the box. I can't help bursting into laughter as I find a necklace with a pendant hanging from it. I lift the heart with the SW in the center out of the box as I continue to laugh.

"I knew you would find the humor," Jack chuckles.

"Will you put it on for me?"

"You don't have to wear it. I don't want you to feel like there are three of us in this relationship."

"I feel nothing of the sort. I want to honor a dying wish. No one else ever has to know what it means. It's a nice gift.

"I can tell Lisa put thought into it. She was a huge part of your life. If I'm going to love you, I want to love all of you. I thank her for inviting me into a part of you you could have easily closed me out of. I feel more connected to you, does that make sense?"

"Yeah, darlin'. It does," he chokes out.

He rounds the table to place the chain around my neck. I smile as he kisses the side of my neck once the necklace falls into place. Brushing my hair out of the way, he continues his trail of kisses, flicking his tongue out against my skin.

"Jack," I breathe.

"I want you, Coral. I've missed you. If you're not ready, I'll stop but I want you something awful bad right now," he groans in my ear as he cups my breasts.

"I want you too."

He lifts me from my seat and turns me in his arms. Then he crushes his lips to mine in a deep and demanding kiss. It's as if we never took a break.

The passion is still there as hot and fierce as ever. Yet it does feel like something has changed. I can tell Jack isn't holding back the way he used to.

I hadn't realized how much he did hold back before. However, now it's clear he did have some reservations in the past. Not anymore.

"Jack," I yelp as he lifts me onto the table and lowers to his knees.

He then peels my panties down my legs and pockets them. I stare down my body at him amused. A smile comes to my lips as I see the determination in his eyes.

"Oh God."

I throw my head back as he buries his face into my core. He's eating my pussy like he can get the time we've lost back through his mouth. Pushing my fingers into his hair, I ride his face for everything I'm worth.

He hums into me as he reaches up to cover my breast with his hand and squeezes. My thighs start to shake, and my juices are dripping into my crack. Suddenly, he pulls back and looks up at me.

"Are you all right? How's your wrist? Is this too much for you?"

"I'm fine. Don't stop, please," I pant.

He gives me a grin and returns to his task without breaking eye contact with me. There's a sparkle in his eyes that I've never seen before. There's something playful and mischievous about it.

I smile back at him and lift a brow. He shakes his head but doesn't stop eating. Instead, he groans and pushes in deeper.

I'm in pure bliss as he makes me come twice more. When he lifts to his feet, his face is glistening from my juices. Leaning in, he then captures my lips in an all-consuming kiss.

"I love you," he says into my mouth.

"I love you too," I whimper. "Maybe we should head to the house."

"I don't have that kind of patience right now," he grunts.

Jack

Coral's place has a full house between Cash and my boys and her girls. However, that's not the reason I'm not moving this to a more secure and private location.

I've been missing my woman, and I can't wait another minute to be inside her. Coral is amazing. I wasn't sure how she would react to Lisa's gift. I honestly wasn't expecting her to see the humor or good intention in it.

I wouldn't have been upset if she didn't want the necklace or decided not to wear it. My fifty-one years have taught me chronological age does not equate to maturity. Coral's response not only turned me on, it was the response of a real woman.

One who can process her own feelings and understand those of her man. It makes me want to be a better man for her.

I intend to allow myself to heal to give her what she needs and deserves. I'll never forget Lisa, but I haven't been this happy in a long time. I can talk and laugh with Coral.

Her big heart makes me want to do more for the community we live in. I've fallen in love with Spring Valley all over again as I see it through Coral and her girls' eyes. Her zeal for life gets my blood pumping.

"We can't, Jack. Not here," Coral moans as I begin to unfasten my belt.

"I don't see why not. We're both adults and I own the place," I reply.

I place her on her feet and turn her around. Her back facing my front. Planting my palm in the center of her back, I push until she's bent over the table.

Bunching her dress up in my hands, I position it over her waist until her ass is in full view. Her pussy glistens back at me, taunting me for my attention. I'm too hard to drop to my knees for another taste.

"I need you now," I groan as I plunge into her tight heat.

"Jack, yes, I've missed you so much. Yes."

"That's it. Keep taking me just like that," I groan as I watch her ass bounce against me.

I smooth my hands over her ass and up her side beneath her dress. She feels so damn good. The sound of her keening and her wet pussy are driving me crazy.

Working my body against hers, I quickly get my shirt off and toss it aside. I need better traction so I get my shoes off and kick out of one leg of my pants. Widening my stance, I bend my knees and keep thrusting.

"Fuck, Coral. Shit, you're so wet."

"You're so deep, Jack. I'm going to come. Yes."

I slap her ass and watch it ripple. I can't help biting my lip as pleasure rocks through me. Grasping her waist, I keep thrusting while pulling her to me.

My eyes roll back in my head. Leaning over her body, I begin to kiss her neck before I suck her flesh into my mouth. She tastes so good.

Her screams get louder as I begin to swivel my hips as I rock into her. Coral begins to clench her magic pussy around me, and I know I'm not going to last much longer.

Sweat is dripping down my face and back. My heart is pounding, and my breathing is heavy, but the connection I have with this woman keeps me grounded to the here and now.

"You feel that? You see how hard you make me? Come for me, baby girl. Come for me now."

I rub her clit as I rock us both to our finish. Coral is lying flat across the table at this point, and I have my chest pressed against her. This feels like where I'm meant to be.

CHAPTER TWENTY-ONE

Progress

Jack

"Hey, Pop. What time did you get in last night?" Hershel asks as he comes from the kitchen with a half-eaten apple in his hand.

I'm at the front desk sorting out check outs and tasks that need doing before the new arrivals get in. We have a full house once again. There's a wedding party coming in.

The wedding will take place in our barn. One of Chance's new ideas for business. Everything has been going well so far.

"When I got in," I murmur.

"I didn't see Miss Coral come in before I left Willowbrook, that's all."

"Good morning," Coral sings as she comes downstairs right as I open my mouth to reply.

"*Oh,*" Hershel drags out. "Now I get it. Minding my business."

"Good, that's the best thing for you."

"Good morning, Miss Coral. Nice to see you. Can I get you some breakfast?"

"I've got her. Why don't you go on and get these rooms ready. I'll check on the party plans in a bit."

"I think Chance already has it covered. He's really into all this, you know. Proud of him. I'll handle the rooms, Pop. Don't worry about it."

Hershel walks off whistling. I shake my head and turn my attention to Coral. She comes to my side, and I wrap my arms around her.

I can't help the smile that comes to my face. That light she has is shining bright this morning. She had suggested going back to her place last night, but I wanted to come back here to the B&B.

I needed to prove to myself that I meant it when I said I was ready. Sleeping in my bed with Coral in my arms brought me more peace than I thought it would. I woke feeling recharged and ready to see what the future will bring.

"How did you sleep?" I ask as I cup her face and run my thumb across her cheek.

"Better than ever. How about you?"

"Better than I have in a long time."

"How can I help? What needs to be done?"

"You can go sit in the dining room and wait for me to bring you breakfast. You're not cleared for work for another week." I peck her lips and give her a good squeeze.

"I'm capable of helping out." She pouts.

"Maybe, but you're not going to. We have it covered. Let me get you fed, and I'll take you to the house. You might need to check that it's still standing."

She laughs and hugs me to her. "My girls know better than to make me hurt them. They may be mischievous at heart, but they'd never allow anyone else to tear my place up."

I join in on her laughter as I lean in to nuzzle her neck and then move to rub the tip of my nose against hers. This moment feels perfect.

ORPHAN HOLD
DO NOT SHIP

H1 – 000000000266

ISBN 9781941924365

CLIENT	Alternate Sourcing
STATION	TPP Receiving Station 03
HELD	2026 – 10 – 08 08:53

SHELF

If its order arrives, scan this label at a receiving station.

"Uncle Jack, Miss Coral, just the two people I've been looking for," Cash says as he walks through the door.

"Hey, Mayor?"

"Uncle Jack," Cash says, rolling his eyes. "Listen, Tom Capepulton wants to sell his land. He came down to my office to let me know before going to Betty-Lou to list.

"We still have funds to acquire the land, but I wanted to see if either of you would make the purchase."

"Did you ever find out where your father got the tip from?" Coral asks.

"You know, I've been thinking about that and trying to figure it out. He sure was pissed off when he came up empty handed and the committee dropped the investigation. Business has been going so well for everyone in town, no one was willing to back his witch hunt," Cash replies.

"That's good to hear. I'll make the purchase. I should probably mention that Alice has been talking about selling a lot more lately as well. She and JC have spoken a few times about it.

"Business has turned around in the best way for her, but she wants to sell to someone younger who will give the same love and care to the place," Coral says.

"Is JC interested?" Cash asks with curiosity in his eyes.

"I don't know. She's mentioned it a few times. Especially after the accident. If you haven't noticed all three of them have been here a lot more. Trust me, it's not all about helping you and the town."

"That's good to know," Cash says and pats his belly. "I'll need to hit the gym more or start volunteering around here in the brewery house more than once a week but JC owning that place would definitely be welcomed."

I chuckle and Coral shakes her head. I had no idea JC was thinking about buying Alice's place. However, it would be a nice fit.

Alice might run it as a bakery, but I still remember the days when Shelby's was open for a full dinner services. My parents used to take me there all the time.

"Well, I'll let Mr. Capepulton know he has a buyer. I think that will cover the larger properties in town for a while," Cash says.

"So you're not as worried about the houses and other smaller properties?"

"No, they would need to change the zoning for the houses and many of the smaller lots. Too much red tape and money to turn their profits quickly and if they don't own lands like this one or Mr. Capepulton's then they can't achieve the luxury destination they're hoping for."

Coral nods her head. I can see the wheels turning. I know she's coming up with something her and her little miracle makers are going to make happen.

I love watching her mind work. She opens her mouth to say something, but Cash holds his hand up as he pulls his phone from his pocket. Coral purses her lips and looks up at me.

"I need to go. Dad had Emma this weekend. He needs me to pick her back up. Thanks again, I'll be in touch soon," Cash says.

"If you need some help with Emma, I can take her. I know Mel is at your office. I can help keep Emma out of your hair for a bit," Coral offers.

"Aw shit," Cash groans and looks down at his watch. "Excuse my language. I should have been there over an hour ago. I can't even blame the woman if she chews me out this time.

"Thanks, but I've got it. Emma might be my saving grace. Mel never gives me the what for when she's around. I'll at least have enough time to buy lunch and explain to smooth things over."

"Mm," Coral and I hum at the same time.

Cash points at us. "I don't have time to ask what that's about. I'll see you guys later. Thanks again."

"They act like a married couple," I murmur once he's out of earshot.

Coral laughs. "I was thinking the same thing. She's taken over running his life and I don't think either of them realizes it. It's quite comical if you ask me."

"You want to tell me over breakfast what you were about to say to Cash. I could see the wheels turning."

"Oh, something Cash said got me to thinking. Ralph once mentioned a case where the zoning locked the developer out of the neighborhood. I was just wondering with all the farms and wildlife parks could you guys zone most of the town to keep out the developer and keep anyone from buying and changing the purpose of the land."

"Not a bad idea. You think he should give Ralph a call and ask for a consult?"

"I think he should ask Mel to talk to her uncle. Ralph will go above and beyond to give her all the answers she needs to move mountains for Cash."

"I'll send him a text. Let's go eat."

Coral

"Wow, that was a lot of fun," I laugh as Jack drops me home from the wedding over at the brewery.

"I'm real proud of Chance. He pulled off a wonderful event for those folks."

"The bride was certainly happy. The father of the bride looked like he had a time."

"Sure did. That man could drink with the best of them." Jack frowns.

"Thinking about tweaking a few details of the events?" I snicker.

"Is it that obvious?"

"Just a little." I hold up two fingers to demonstrate.

He chuckles. "Enough about that place and business. My feet are hurting from all that dancing. How about we try for that bath again?"

"Sounds good to me. I had planned to take one and read a book before you mentioned coming over for the night."

"Sounds good. You mind if I make myself useful and read to you?"

"Nope, I don't mind at all."

As we enter my bedroom, I head into the bathroom and start the tub. I make quick work of filling the tub with water and bubble bath. Once done, I turn to head back into the bedroom to undress and grab my book.

However, I come face to face with a naked Jack as he holds up the book from my nightstand. A grin comes to my lips. I give him a nod as I begin to slip out of my dress.

"This what you wanted to read?"

"It is." I crook my finger for him to come closer as I back up toward the tub.

"Slow down, darlin'," Jack calls out as he rushes forward and wraps his arm around me.

"I'm fine. You've been fussing over me all day."

"Can you blame me for wanting to make sure the woman I love is safe from harm."

"No, I guess not. Especially not when you say it like that while having that look in your eyes. Come on big guy. Let's get in and relax."

He steps into the water first, then helps me to get in next. He sits and I take the space between his legs. This bathtub is one of my favorite parts of this house.

With Jack inside with me, it's the perfect fit. I settle against his chest and we both sigh. I close my eyes and snuggle in closer to him.

"Should I start where you have this bookmark?"

"That's fine," I say without opening my eyes.

He begins to read as I get lost in his deep melodic voice. I don't know when, but I fall right to sleep as he reads. I wake to his soft lips against my shoulder.

"Hey there, should I add some warm water or are you ready to get out?"

"Um, oh. Did I fall asleep?"

"You did. You must have been tired. It was a really good book. I'll have to borrow it when you're finished."

I snicker. "It is a good one. Been waiting a while for it to come out. The first one was just as good."

"You never did tell me how you became a librarian."

"My father was a teacher. I used to go to parent-teacher night with him. I would always sit in the library while he met with the parents.

"I fell in love with that place. The books were like friends. Mrs. Doran. That was the librarian's name. She would help me find books to read and let me take them home. Daddy would take them back when I was finished.

"That always stuck with me. After college the profession made sense. That's actually how I met Ralph. He used to study in the library I worked at," I tell him.

"What did your mama do? Are your parents still around?"

"My mother was a doctor. They're both still alive and kicking. I think JC and Mel got their traveling spirits from those two. They've been in Japan this year. I'm sure you'll meet them when they get back."

"The closest I can get you to meeting my folks are the archives in the library."

"Archives?"

"There are books on my family and this land in the archives. They go back generations. Ask Flo about them."

"That's so interesting. I'll have to check that out."

A chill runs through me, causing me to shiver. Jack tightens his hold around me and kisses the top of my head. I look up at him and smile.

"Come on. Let's get you warm and in the bedroom."

I yawn. "Great idea."

CHAPTER TWENTY-TWO

Special Surprise

Jack

"Relax, Pop. You're sweating your shirt out. You're totally going to give it away," Chance whispers as he walks over to me in the kitchen where I'm starting to freak out.

We're all at Coral's for a game night. Chance and Hershel hired some more help at the B&B to give us all more time to ourselves.

On nights like this it's been a real help. We're only a call away but we can focus on time together and with those we care about. Time to do special things for them.

Like surprises. Surprises like the one I have planned for my Coral tonight. Everyone's in on this one.

"What if she doesn't like it?" I murmur to Chance.

He tugs me into a hug. "She's going to love it, Dad. Everything is going to be fine as long as you stop acting all weird," he whispers in my ear.

I sigh as he releases me. Looking at my armpits, I then groan. My shirt is soaked through.

Jo comes over and wraps her arms around my waist. I look down at her and she's smiling up at me. Wrapping an arm around her, I give a gentle squeeze.

"You are so adorable. I love how you love my mom. It's cute that you're so nervous but I've also seen this alpha side of you that's willing to take care of Mom. Relax, we have your back," she says.

I give her a wink. "Thanks. We should all get back to it."

Jo releases me and gives my arm a squeeze. We all make our way back into the living room where a lively game of charades is in progress. I can't help the smile that comes to my face.

I give Hershel a nod to let him know I'm ready. The goal tonight is for Coral to win all the activities. The prize will be the surprise I have for her.

"Okay, guys. Let's switch things up. How about a game of Family Freud," Hershel croons.

"Sounds great. Mom, you're on our team," JC says.

Coral laughs. "That's not fair. They don't stand a chance."

"You know we don't do losing," Mel says and pulls a face.

"Well bring it on," Cash chuckles.

I give him a look, knowing how competitive he is. He pulls a long face and gives me a nod to let me know he's not going to ruin this. I shake my head and snort.

We get the game going and just as Coral and the girls said they would, they whip our asses. It's actually comical. We don't have to throw the game one bit, we're just that bad.

"Aw, Cash, honey. Don't look so sad," Coral coos as we lose for the second time in a row.

"Yeah, yeah," he mumbles.

"Good job, ladies. How about we take a look at the prize for the evening," I say.

"Prize?" Coral asks with a look of confusion on her face.

"Yeah, Mom. We agreed the winners would get a prize. I think you were in the bathroom or something," Mel says.

"Oh, this has been so much fun," Coral replies.

I go over and offer Coral my hand. With a smile, she takes it and stands. Placing her hand in the crook of my arm, I walk her toward the front door where Chance and Hershel have already disappeared.

The girls and Cash are all behind us chattering quietly. My heart is racing. I don't realize I'm holding my breath until Coral gasps at my side.

Chance has turned on the engine and headlights, illuminating the night. I look down at Coral and she's looking back at me with awe in her expression.

"Surprise," everyone calls in unison.

"I don't understand," she says softly.

"I wanted to replace your car. I know you needed a new one, but you've been hesitant because you're still nervous to get back behind the wheel.

"I'm not rushing you. I really enjoy picking you up from work and dropping you off, but I also know how independent you are and see your frustration when you have to ask to go places you would normally take yourself. I want to help you get pass this.

"You do so much for everyone else. This is me doing for you. This SUV will get you around safely and give us both peace of mind. It has driver assist so if you have an accident or get stuck somewhere, they'll get you help right away," I say as I look into her eyes.

"You bought me a car?"

"Yeah, Mom, he did," Jo says happily. "Fussed about the brand, color, and make. It was so cute."

"Do you like it?" I ask as I blush while waiting for her answer.

Coral

"I love it," I breathe as I lift up on my toes and pull his head down for our lips to meet.

I peck his lips repeatedly as I hold him in place. I can't believe he bought me a car. I had planned to get a new one but he's right, I have been procrastinating. That incident scared the mess out of me.

I love that he has seen how I feel and has taken the initiative to give me a little push. I didn't want to worry the girls with my reluctance, and I didn't want to fall into my own head, but I still haven't mentioned how I feel to anyone, and I planned to put it off for as long as I could.

"I think that's our cue, everyone. Hersh, you still offering those beers tonight?" Mel calls out as Jack palms the back of my head to deepen the kiss.

"Yup, you ladies packed your bags? I have a suite at the B&B ready for you too."

"We're ready to go. Our work is done here," Jo sings.

"Here's the key, Pop," Chance chuckles.

Jack doesn't break the kiss as he takes the key from Chance while he continues to devour my mouth. I pull away from Jack and chuckle as I look around and find my girls climbing into the cars with Chance, Hershel, and Cash. Jack pushes my hair aside and kisses my neck. The rumbling sound he makes vibrates through my body.

"Jack," I yelp as he tosses me over his shoulder and starts for the house.

He gives a chuckle and slaps my ass but doesn't stop moving. I cling to the back of his shirt as he moves through the house. A smile comes to my lips as I focus on his cute tight ass.

A laugh bursts from my lips as he drops me on the bed with a bounce. I lift a brow at him as he begins unbuttoning his shirt. I laugh harder as I begin to realize why he's been sweating so much tonight.

I had assumed he was flustered with game night. Now I get that he was nervous about my gift. This fact only endears him to me more.

"Let me help you with that," I purr as he goes to release his belt.

Sitting up on the bed, I lean forward and unfasten his belt for him. I have been a lucky woman in my life. My ex-husband and my current man have been some fine men and well endowed.

My mouth waters at the sight of Jack's still toned V. Pushing down his pants, I reveal his thick thighs and strong legs. His penis is at full attention, pointing right at me as I free him from his boxer briefs.

"Oh God, baby girl. I love when you do that," Jack groans as I drop to the floor and take him into my mouth.

I hum in pleasure as I bob my head and get my hands involved. Jack widens his stance and places his hand on his back as if he needs the extra support. I place one hand on his thigh and begin to rub up and down his leg.

It's one of the little things I've learn that turns him on. Looking up at him through my lashes, I see the pleasure in his expression. I double my efforts wanting to give him something for being so sweet and caring.

"Oh shit, Coral. I need you now."

Before I can respond, he pulls from my mouth and lifts me into his arms. He then climbs onto the bed with me in his hold. Swiftly, he peels me from my clothes and covers my body with his.

"Jack," I moan as he pushes into me.

He captures my lips in a slow, searing kiss. I cling to his shoulders as he slowly rocks into me. He breaks the kiss to look in my eyes as he makes love to me.

I lock my legs around his waist and throw my head back into the pillow. He reaches for my hands and locks our fingers together as his slow strokes make my toes curl. I'm getting so wet for him.

I look up at the ceiling and get lost in the sound of his moans and groans as we move in sync with each other. I honestly didn't think I would find this once Ralph and I separated.

Now all I want is to fully embrace this feeling, this sense of peace. It's like I've found the person for my now. I don't know that my younger self would have been ready for Jack, but this Coral, the woman I am now, she's made for this Jack.

Our love proves that love has all types of forms and comes right when it's needed. This … this love is undeniable. I feel a soul deep connection with Jack that causes me to wake ready to chose him each day.

"I love you," he groans in my ear.

"I love you too."

Courtland

"What was so important you needed to talk to me now?" I bite out as I walk into the secluded building I was asked to come to.

"Did I or did I not tell you not to let it get back that I gave you that tip."

"What are you talking about, Betty-Lou? I haven't told anyone anything. If it got out there it didn't come from me."

"Well, we have a big fucking problem. People are asking questions, and my name is starting to come up. You do understand why this is a huge problem, don't you?"

"A problem for you, yes. You are the one who went behind my back to make your own connection with the developers. Guess, you didn't do any research into who they were in the first place.

"I've always kept my distance from them because I knew from the beginning, they were the mob. Looks like you didn't find that out until after you had a knife in my back.

"Now, this all falls on you, doesn't it? You haven't been able to deliver on any of your backstabbing promises, am I right? I never needed you, Betty-Lou.

"You needed me. Now you're in deep shit and you want to drag me into it. Well, you know what? I haven't gotten what I want yet. So this ship is going down, but not with me," I say smugly.

"Courtland, you asshole. I need you to call Cash off. Tell him to stop whatever he's doing. They will kill me. This is not a joke."

"You should have thought about that before your greedy ass tried to fuck me over."

"I thought you were going to screw me out of the deal. What does it matter now, it doesn't look like any of it is going to come through and now, I'm fucked for what?" She hisses.

"I could give two shits. You've put my son in danger with your antics. I'll have to clean up your mess as it is. You get your name out of their mouths yourself. I'm done."

"Ugh, fuck you. I hope everything falls apart for you. Don't think I'm not going to expose you after this. You can't have your cake and eat it too. I'll make sure Cash knows everything," Betty-Lou growls and storms out.

She doesn't even wait to lock this place back up. I shrug and pull my phone to send a text. As I'm looking down at my phone and walking out the door, the loud sound of a collision and screeching tires grabs my attention.

I look up and find Betty-Lou lying crumpled in the middle of the street. I grunt and turn to head in the opposite direction. This is none of my business and I'm not sticking around to be next.

"Dumb ass woman," I mumble as I rush away.

CHAPTER TWENTY-THREE

Next Chapter

Coral

The next year …

"Hey, there, Coral," Alice sings as she walks over to where I'm nursing a beer while watching all the dancing. "Now this is just what the town needed."

"Yes, it is."

This past year has been more than eventful. So much craziness and change. There was Betty-Lou's unsolved hit and run, the investigation into Cash and the mayor's office, and some guy who tried to stake a claim on Terry and Jack's land. If I hadn't already been deep in the archives reading about the town and the original families he might have gotten away with it.

However, we put a stop to that. Mel was Cash's saving grace. She tightened that office up so much, when they did investigate, they couldn't find a single thing out of place.

Instead, they found out that there were things amiss in other areas that Cash and his office had no hands-on control over. We're still awaiting more details on that and a final outcome. Unfortunately, Betty-Lou's situation doesn't have any positive details.

She was in a coma and didn't recover. They said she was in the street for too long without medical attention. If the person who hit her would have gotten her some help or if she would have been found sooner, she might have had a different outcome.

No one knows what happened. At least, no one has come forward. I never liked the woman, but I hate what happened to her. As a town, everyone has come together to support Mayor Cash, Jack, and Terry.

I'm so excited for tonight. The brewery is throwing a Christmas party for everyone. The locals and anyone else who wants to join the festivities are welcome.

The music has kept the dance floor full, and the raffle tables have been busy. Chance and Jo did a good job. I wasn't involved in this one.

Not that I didn't want to help. I've just been busy with so many other things like running fundraisers and learning more about running the brewery and B&B from Jack. Speaking of Jack, I look around to see where he has gotten off to.

I wouldn't mind dancing with him again. We've been having such a good night. Yesterday was an emotional day for us.

Jack asked me to remove Lisa's gift to me. I did and we took the necklace out by the lake on the property where we buried it. I think I cried more than he did, but I could see in his eyes he was ready.

I don't know what prompted the request, but he's been in a great mood today. I don't think I've ever seen him smile so much. Within the last year, we've grown so much closer as a couple.

Actually, we've grown as a family. My girls spend more time here then they do back home in the city. I left them the house back in the city, but I don't think it feels like home to them anymore.

That would explain a lot of the changes. Jack and I had a bet going on which would move here permanently first. To my surprise I lost.

Chance and Jo are like two peas in a pod. They've become the best of friends. JC and Alice came to an agreement that works for them. Mel … Mel is Mel and she's always taking me by surprise.

The loud pitch of someone tapping a mic and the speakers squealing grabs my attention. I look toward the stage to find Jack standing up there. I smile, he looks extra handsome tonight.

He's dressed in all black and has on one of his big old cowboy belt buckles. My smile widens when he takes off his black Stetson. His barber has been doing something new with his hair. I like it on him.

"Good evening, folks. Thank you all for coming out. Wow, there's a lot of you.

"Well, I guess that just makes this night more special. As many of you know, one of the most wonderful women in the world entered our town and took over my heart.

"It was love at first sight for me. I didn't think my heart would beat for another woman after losing my wife, but there she was the spark who brought it all back to me and this place. Coral, darlin', will you come up here?"

I place my beer mug down and walk slowly toward the stage as I eye Jack warily. When I get up on stage, he wraps an arm around my waist and pecks me on the lips. Clearing his throat, he releases me and drops to one knee.

"This place hasn't been filled with this much love in years. We were too busy hurting. Now, my boys smile more, we all laugh more and I know it's because of you. You've taught me to love again.

"You've given me a second chance. Shown me love doesn't have to end or die with the part of us we lose. I've learned that I don't have to forget my past to enjoy my present and future, but I can move forward into this next chapter.

"So I'm asking, will you move forward with me, Coral? Will you marry me?"

"Yes," I choke out. "Yes."

Jack

"That was some party, Uncle Jack," Cash says as Coral and I dance on the dance floor.

There's no more music. The band packed up and left about twenty minutes ago. However, this is where it feels right to be. Me and my woman pressed heart to heart.

"You and Emma heading home?"

"Yeah, she's out for the count. She had a ball."

"Glad to hear that. Tonight was a great success. We might have to make the Christmas party a standing tradition."

"Mel and Jo just said the same thing. It's not a bad idea. I was thinking—"

"Cash, I need to speak with you."

Cash purses his lips as his mother calls after him. I try not to laugh. I don't envy him one bit. That woman can drive anyone crazy.

Cash excuses himself and Coral and I continue to sway. I close my eyes and send up a prayer of thanks.

"Will we live at the inn or Willowbrook?" Coral asks suddenly.

"That's up to you. We can live at Willowbrook full time with all the new staff. I think it's time I retire anyway. Chance has been doing a fine job, I think it's time he takes the reins full time."

"Are you sure?"

"It's not like I'll give up working here all together. This place is in my blood."

"Well, I'm fine either way. Although, I do think Chance will do great things with this place. He already has," she says.

Suddenly Jo runs across the barn house and out the door. Coral and I pull apart and look after her. Coral goes to take a step forward, but Chance stumbles into view.

"Jo, wait," he calls out.

"Ut-oh."

"You can say that again," I chuckle and shake my head.

ABOUT THE AUTHOR

Blue Saffire, award-winning, bestselling author of over eighty contemporary romance novels and novellas, writes with the intention to touch the heart and the mind. Blue hooks, weaves, and loops multiple series, keeping you engaged in her worlds. Blue writes for her own publishing company, Perceptive Illusions as Blue Saffire, as well as Royal Blue.

Blue and her husband live in a house filled with laughter and creativity in Long Island, NY. Both working hard to build the Blue brand and cultivate their love for the arts. Creative is their family affair.

Blue holds an MBA in Marketing and Project Management, as well as an MED in Instructional Technology and Curriculum Design. She is also an NLP Master Practitioner.

ACKNOWLEDGMENTS

How many of you remembered the beginning of this one from the challenge I did a few years back? It spoke to me, and I had to write them a book. Actually, a series because everyone came up with a voice. Jack and Coral were sweet.

There are so many things still to come from this family and Spring Valley. I hope you're enjoying getting to know them. Look forward for more soon.

As always, my dear reader friends, thank you so much for your continued support and patience. I know you have waited for a new exclusive for a whole. We back. LOL.

Thank you for the encouraging reviews, emails, videos, posts, shares, comments, and DMs. Big thanks, friends. Remember, sharing is caring. If you have a friend who reads, let them know about me, please.

Shout out to my husband. He's watching me do a lot and cheering me on while I do it. It's better to be surrounded by people who talk to you truthfully and with encouragement. Thanks, boo.

As always, all thanks be to the source of it all. God has given me this gift and I'm grateful to grow and nature it. Walking in faith looks different to everyone. I'm grateful for my view.

It's my season and I'm claiming it. Always grateful and thankful to God. I give Him all the glory. I love you with all my heart and thank you for continuing to bless me, this pen, and this journey. Continuously unapologetically blessed and highly favored.

Next! Let's get to know Chance and Jo.

Wait, there is more to come! You can stay updated with my latest releases, learn more about me, the author, and be a part of contests by subscribing to my newsletter at

www.BlueSaffire.com

If you enjoyed *Heart to Heart*, I'd love to hear

your thoughts and please feel free to leave a

review on my website. And when you do, please let me

know by emailing me TheBlueSaffire@gmail.com

or leave a comment on Facebook https://www.facebook.com/BlueSaffireDiaries or Twitter @TheBlueSaffire

Other books by Blue Saffire

Placed in Best Reading Order

Also available ...

Legally Bound

Legally Bound 2: Against the Law

Legally Bound 3: His Law

Perfect for Me

Hush 1: Family Secrets

Ballers: His Game

Brothers Black 1: Wyatt the Heartbreaker

Legally Bound 4: Allegations of Love

Hush 2: Slow Burn

Legally Bound 5.0: Sam

Yours 1: Losing My Innocence

Yours 2: Experience Gained

Yours 3: Life Mastered

Ballers 2: His Final Play

Legally Bound 5.1: Tasha Illegal Dealings

Brothers Black 2: Noah

Legally Bound 5.2: Camille

Legally Bound 5.3 & 5.4 Special Edition

Where the Pieces Fall

Legally Bound 5.5: Legally Unbound

Brothers Black 4: Braxton the Charmer

Broken Soldier

Brothers Black 5: Felix the Watcher

A Home for Christmas

Doctor Feel Good

Brothers Black 6: Ryan the Joker

Brothers Black 7: Johnathan the Fixer

Wild Hearts

Pieces of Trevor's Heart

Ballers 3: His Team

Ronan Book 1: Kings of New York

Dylan Book 2: Kings of New York

Coming Soon…
King of Gods Book 4: Immortal Iron Brothers Series
King of Past Book 5: Immortal Iron Brothers Series
Brooklyn Book 3: Kings of New York Series

Other Blue Saffire Series

Hold On To Me Series
My Funny Valentine
Be My Valentine

Hitter Squad Series
Remember Me

Work Husband Series
Unexpected Lovers
My Best Friend's Wish
The Ones Left Behind
The Last Ones Standing

The Lost Souls MC Series
Forever
Never
Always

The Moran Brothers Series
Love Notes
Stay With Me

The Ahole Club Series**
Pit Book 1: The A**hole Club
Ox Book 5: The A**hole Club
Kelex Book 6: The A**hole Club

Immortal Iron Brothers Series
King of Knights Book 1
King of Inferno Book 2
King of Tides Book 3

Check out Blue Saffire exclusives on the
BlueSaffire.com website
The Fixer
His Miracle Baby

Dark Disciples Series
Razor
Dane
Trip

Discipline Disciples Series
Wounded
12 Rounds

Bay Breezes Series
Professor Jones
Room 112

Love's Brew Series
Heart to Heart
Bear With Me coming soon …

Other books from Evei Lattimore Collection Books by Blue Saffire
Black Bella 1

Destiny 1: Life Decisions
Destiny 2: Decisions of the Next Generation
Destiny 3 coming soon…

Star

Other books from Royal Blue Gay Romance Collection written by Blue Saffire
Kyle's Reveal
Beau's Redemption

www.ingramcontent.com/pod-product-compliance
Lightning Source LLC
Chambersburg PA
CBHW061553250926
52052CB00010B/3187
9781941924365